Unlocked

The Men of Bolt Corporation

Book Three

K.A. Wombolt

Contents

Unlocked

Dedication

Tr!gger Warnings:

Book Tropes:

Chapter 1	1
Chapter 2	6
Chapter 3	9
Chapter 4	12
Chapter 5	16
Chapter 6	20
Chapter 7	25
Chapter 8	35
Chapter 9	40
Chapter 10	47
Chapter 11	49
Chapter 12	55
Chapter 13	58
Chapter 14	60
Chapter 15	64
Chapter 16	71

Chapter 17	79
Chapter 18	82
Chapter 19	85
Chapter 20	91
Chapter 21	96
Chapter 22	105
Chapter 23	109
Chapter 24	113
Chapter 25	118
Chapter 26	122
Chapter 27	126
Chapter 28	129
Chapter 29	133
Chapter 30	138
Chapter 31	143
Chapter 32	146
Chapter 33	150
Chapter 34	155
Chapter 35	158
Chapter 36	164
Chapter 37	168
Chapter 38	172
Chapter 39	178
Chapter 40	180
Chapter 41	184
Chapter 42	187
Chapter 43	190
Chapter 44	192

Epilogue	195
Author Note	199

Dedication

You're such a good girl, aren't you?
You would do anything we ask,
my perfect, Pretty Girl.

But you're a bad little slut too.
Always greedy and ready to do what you're told,
aren't you, Kitten?

Now turn the fucking page.
You know you want to…

Tr!gger Warnings:

R@pe (Non-Con)
Dub-Con
M*rder
Harassment
@buse (S*xual, Emotional & Physical)
Assault
De@th/Grief
Child SA flashbacks
Stalking
T0rture
S*xually Explicit Scenes
K!dnapping
F0rced Drug @buse
Mental Health
BDSM
Found Family
Slavery
Traff!cking
Betrayal
Toxic Behaviors
Misogyny
Graphic Vi0lence
Slut Shaming
Bullying
Abandonment
Adoption
Blackmail
Gun Vi0lence
Kn!fe Vi0lence

Book Tropes:

Why Choose?
Enemies to Lovers
MFM
Alpha Male
Sweet/Gentle Male
Tattooed and Pierced
Dark Romance
Dual/Multi POV
First Person POV
HEA
Workplace Romance
Billionaire Romance
Mafia Romance
Morally Grey MMC
Possessive MMC
Power Imbalance- Boss/Employee
Praise Kink
Degradation Kink
Love Triangle
Touch her and D!e
Tortured Hero
Tortured Heroine
Forced Proximity
Friends with Benefits
Independent/Sassy FMC
Love Triangle
Secret Relationship
BDSM
Double Penetration
Instalove
Found Family

Chapter 1

Jamison
Eight years old

"Come outside and play catch with me," Jonathan begs from the doorway as he pushes a brown lock of hair from his eyes. He's rolling a battered baseball back and forth between both hands.

"I'd prefer not," I reply to him as I flip the page of my book. I stole it from Aunt Greta's bookshelf last month and have read it at least ten times. She has an entire shelf with her "special" books that she lets none of us children touch. I regularly sneak in and switch out my books after finishing them. I'm careful to keep a children's book close by whenever I am reading so she doesn't catch me. My current book is a Stephen King novel called *The Dark Half*. I rarely reread a book this many times, but the storyline is quite fascinating.

I look up at my twin, who still hasn't left the doorway, and ponder what it would have been like if one of us absorbed the other in utero. Maybe if Jonathan had absorbed me, he would have been adopted a long time ago. Aunt Greta doesn't say it, but I know it's true. I've overheard the many potential parents who come by in hopes of adopting children here. And I've listened to her on the phone, telling others she's 'not sure' about me. A memory sucks me in from just a few weeks before.

"We had another couple come by this week," Aunt Greta says over the phone. "They loved Jonathan, but his brother...well, they couldn't understand how identical twins could be so different." She sighs and nods before continuing, "He's been like this since they landed on our front steps as newborns. He never smiled or laughed.

He never even cried!" She goes silent while listening to the other person speak. "I can't split them up. The couple asked, and I denied them, so they chose that little boy Jeremy instead. At this point, I'm assuming they will stay here forever. You know how hard it is to find families willing to take children after age five. They are well past that already."

I'm jolted out of my memory by the feel of my mattress dipping. Jonathan stares at me with his bright blue eyes, the only difference in our looks. While his are bright and blue like the sky, mine are deep blue like the ocean's darkest depths.

"Where did you go?" he asks me quietly.

"Nowhere," I reply, eyeing the ball he is still fidgeting with. "You don't even have a glove."

"I found some in a bin out in the shed earlier today. I think they were left here last week. Aunt Greta said we could have them. Please play with me. All the other kids are too small and they don't throw right." He pouts as he pushes his lip out.

I roll my eyes before carefully sticking a small paper in my book to mark my spot.

"Fine," I say as I push off the bed, making Jonathan jump up. I lift my mattress and slide the book under it to hide it from Aunt Greta. "One hour, and then you leave me be for the rest of the day."

My twin smiles wide before yanking me out the door and down the rickety steps of our orphanage. I follow him outside, and we make our way over to the grassy area farther away from the house. We begin to throw the baseball back and forth. A few minutes pass before we hear a car coming down the long dirt road to our home. I see a sleek black car pull right up by the front steps. Aunt Greta runs down the steps of our house, looking extremely flustered, before stopping in front of the car. A man and woman both step out and around to the front of the car before stopping in front of Aunt Greta.

"Who do you think they are?" my brother asks curiously. "They look rich."

"I'm not sure," I reply as I gaze at them. The man is wearing a suit, and the woman is wearing a pretty flowy dress that hangs just below her knees. I see the jewelry flash on her fingers, ears, and wrist. My brother is correct. They do look rich. The question is, why are they here at an orphanage? Aunt Greta always lets us know ahead of time if a prospective family will be showing up. I break my gaze from the couple just in time to catch the ball my brother throws at me.

"Sorry." he says when he sees me glare at him. "I thought you were ready!"

A few more minutes pass, and the couple still hasn't moved from where they are standing with Aunt Greta.

"We should go over there," Jonathan says as he walks up to me. "Maybe they will like us? We could live in a giant house and ride in a cool car like that."

"I doubt they will want us. They are probably here hoping to get a little girl. I bet that woman already has a closet full of princess dresses ready to go."

"Whatever." he says before taking off towards the couple. I stroll over, giving my twin plenty of time to talk to the friendly couple before I show up and *scare* them away. He is speaking animatedly about his baseball by the time I get there. The couple both smile at him while he talks.

"And who is this?" The woman asks as I approach.

"This is my brother, Jamison," Jonathan replies.

"Pleasure to meet you," I say, shaking her and her husband's hands. The woman furrows her brow and looks towards Aunt Greta, who coughs a little before muttering. "Jamison has a high vocabulary. He reads a lot."

"Well, that is wonderful." the man says as he rubs his wife's back. "Isn't that, honey?"

A look of disgust crosses the woman's face, causing me to narrow my eyes. Jonathan looks at me with pleading eyes. He doesn't need to speak a word and I know what he is saying. My heart sinks a bit. I'm the reason my brother doesn't live in a fancy home with a mom and a dad. I don't want to, but I force a smile onto my face. It feels foreign and fake, and I know I'm not fooling the woman because she doesn't smile back. The man does, though. He beams at me. His large white teeth shine brightly as he squeezes his wife's shoulder.

"They are perfect." he says to Aunt Greta, and her eyes widen.

"Are you sure you don't want to see other children before you decide?" Aunt Greta asks.

The man looks at his wife, who stares at me and then at my brother while biting her bottom lip. I don't like the way she looks at Jonathan. She seems hungry, as if she might devour him any second. The smile from my face drops and I'm ready to grab my brother and run, but the pleading look on his face stops me. He wants this so badly. He wants a family. I don't need anyone but him, but Jonathan…I know he needs more.

The woman looks at her husband and nods.

"Umm, okay," Aunt Greta sighs. "Come with me, Mr. and Mrs. Clark, so we can get the paperwork started. They follow her up the steps and into the house. Once they are out of sight, Jonathan turns to me with excitement.

"We are getting a family!" He squeals before grabbing and dragging me inside and up to our room. I look around the old room, realizing we really have nothing to pack. We have been in this room all our lives, and we have absolutely no personal possessions. My brother lies on his bed and tosses the ball in the air while I make my way to mine. I pull the book out I hid earlier and flop onto the bed, leaning my back against the wall and pulling my knees up. The sound of footsteps walking down the hall causes me to hastily shove the book under my pillow. Aunt Greta appears in our doorway while a group of younger kids run by, screaming and laughing.

"Keep it down," she yells at them as she enters the room and sits on my bed. My brother sits up on his and looks over at her.

"Are you both ready to go?" She asks as she fidgets with my bedsheet.

"Yes," my brother says excitedly.

A look of worry crosses her face before she eyeballs the edge of the book, peeking out from under my pillow.

"I know you have been reading my books, Jamison. I also noticed that a particular one has been missing for a while. Would you like to take it with you?" She smiles, but it doesn't quite reach her eyes.

"I would, yes," I respond to her before tilting my head. "Are you unwell?"

Suddenly, she pulls herself together and sits up straight.

"Of course not, I'm fine. Why wouldn't I be? You guys are finally going to have a home!" Aunt Greta stands up and claps her hands together before ushering us towards the door. "They are ready for you both now."

My brother runs ahead and jogs down the stairs, but Aunt Greta stops me at the top.

"Watch out for your brother, Jamison. Do as Mr. and Mrs. Clark say. They come from a very prestigious family. Their name will take you very far someday."

I nod my head at her and turn, but she grabs me quickly and whispers, "Please be careful, Jamison. Money is the root of all evil."

She disappears down the stairs before I can respond, leaving me completely confused.

Chapter 2

Kaz
Eight years old

"Hey darling, why don't you come sit over here with me?" An old man asks me as I sneak through the tables at Mommy's work. His teeth are crooked and yellow and his nose is big but Mommy always says she has to be nice to the men at work. I want to be like her. She gets to dress up fancy and wear pretty makeup like a princess.

"I'm looking for my Mommy," I reply, in my most grown up voice. "I can't find my crayons and I want to color." I put my hands on my hips and stand up tall, lifting my chin and smiling wide. My lashes flutter just like Mommy when she talks to men.

The old man chuckles and pats his leg. "Come sit here, darling. I'll call someone over to find you some crayons."

He seems so nice and I really do want to color so I hop up on his thigh, wiggling around to get comfortable. He grunts like I hurt him, making me freeze.

"I'm sorry. Did I hurt you?" Maybe he has a bad leg. Our neighbor has a bad leg and she's always walking around with her cane, moaning.

"No, Darling." His voice comes out gruff.

I continue looking around Mommy's work, trying to find her in the crowd of people. My nose scrunches up when I see some of the nice ladies Mommy works with walking around with their boobies showing. Why aren't they wearing the pretty outfits that they got all dressed up in? I turn to see another lady dancing for a man. She's on his lap just like I am, except she is pushing her naked body against him. I look away quickly, embarrassed by what is happening.

"Don't be ashamed, Darling. These beautiful women aren't afraid to do what feels good," the old man whispers in my ear. His breath is hot on my ear and it smells rotten. "Does this feel good?" He asks, rubbing his fingers on my thigh, just below the hem of my dress.

"My tummy hurts," I reply, closing my eyes.

The old man hugs me closer to his body, surrounding me with his bad smell. "Shh, Darling, I'll make you feel better." My eyes snap open when his rough fingers work their way underneath my dress and slide higher.

"I shouldn't be out here. Mommy told me not to leave the room." I try to move off of the old man's lap but he keeps me in place, his grip on me tightening. A lone tear slips down my face just as my eyes connect with Mommy's. She's naked up on a stage. The lights are shining on her brightly, while she dances to the music playing. She looks angry.

Suddenly, I'm ripped from the old man's arms. I look up into the eyes of Miss Mary, Mommy's boss. She looks at me worriedly before glaring at the old man.

"We were just talking," he says, with his hands up.

Miss Mary covers my ears while saying something to him, before carrying me back to the room. "Stay here, Kazzy baby, okay?"

I nod my head and watch her walk out the door. Someone yells on the other side before the door slams open and my Mommy comes in. I run to her with my arms held wide, wanting her comfort. The sound of her slap echoes around the room, and I'm thrown to the floor. Tears fill my eyes and I look up to see her face red and angry.

"You almost got me fired, you little bitch. I told you not to leave this room. Stay here so I can finish my damn shift or next time I'll make sure to leave you with one of those men out there," she gestures behind her with her thumb angrily.

"I'm so-sorry," I try to say, but she's already out the door, leaving the bitter taste of blood in my mouth and a pool of my tears on the floor.

Chapter 3

Jonathan
Twelve years old

I sit across the dining table from my brother, Jamison, while eating my meal. Our adoptive father, Richard, sits at the head of the table while our adoptive mother, Vivian, sits to my right.

"How is your schoolwork going, Jamison?" My father asks my brother.

My brother pushes the corn on his plate back and forth with his fork, with zero emotion on his face.

"Very well, father. All A's. My teachers are providing me with higher-level work now."

"That's fantastic," father says and claps his hands together. "It's about time I introduce you to some of my colleagues. How lucky we are to have chosen two smart and talented children, right, Vivian? A boy genius and a future baseball star."

My mother looks up at Richard and smiles as her hand lands on my leg under the table. "Oh yes, I'm so thrilled. Jonathan's coach told me how well he was doing the other day. He might be a future MLB player. What do you think, Jonathan?" Her hand glides up my thigh, causing my body to stiffen. I sit frozen in my chair as her fingers run towards my inner thigh. "Ya, umm, that would be cool."

I see my brother's eyes narrow in on us, but I don't say anything. I can't let him know I'm the weak link. He has always been the stronger one of us. He can always hide and control his emotions while I have let mine flow freely. My escape has always been through joking around and laughter.

I'm not laughing inside while my adoptive mother inappropriately rubs her hand on my inner thigh, yet I force a smile on my face and laugh anyway. "Wouldn't it be cool if I was a famous pitcher?"

"Yes, it would, son. Yes, it would!" Richard replies.

Vivian's fingers lightly brush closer to my crotch, making me gulp and widen my eyes before scrunching them shut. I count to ten, silently praying she doesn't take this further. What would my father think if he found out she had been sneaking into my room at night? Where would he send us? The orphanage we grew up in burned down shortly after we were adopted. What if he sent us away somewhere worse? At least here, we had everything else we wanted or needed. I could escape inside myself a little longer, and then we could be free. She loves me; that's all this is. She can't help it. Jamison stands up so suddenly that it knocks the table against us and spills our mother's wine. Her hand jolts off my leg and she stands quickly, dabbing her dress with a napkin.

"Sorry," my brother says with zero remorse on his face. "I'm feeling a little unwell. I think I will retire to my room for the rest of the evening."

"I think that is wise," my adoptive mother responds coldly.

My father stands up and presses his hand to Jamison's forehead. "You don't feel warm, but getting a good night's rest is probably best. Go on up. I'll have Deloras clean up this mess."

My brother nods and spins on his heel before heading upstairs. I excuse myself quickly, before following behind him, but stop short when I hear my parents bickering in the dining room. Jamison is already up the stairs and out of sight when I hear pieces of their conversation.

"He did it on purpose…"

"Get yourself together…"

"…Taking them to The Cellar in three weeks."

"…Worth so much money now."

"They are ridiculously handsome…"

"Can you imagine the money?"

I blink in confusion at the last sentence. My parents have loads of money. My father owns multiple large corporations and is extremely well known. He even plans to run for Senate one day. Why would they need more? And what is The Cellar? Afraid I'll get caught if I stay longer, I go upstairs and into my bedroom. Jamison's room is directly across the hall from mine, and his door is already closed. I think about checking on him but decide against it. I don't want to bother him if he really is feeling sick.

After finishing my homework a few hours later, I fall asleep.

The door to my bedroom opens slowly, waking me from my sleep. I peek my eyes open enough to see the time on the clock. It's 2:00 in the morning. I slam my eyes shut, wishing Jamison was still sharing a room with me like we did the first year we were adopted. That ended the first night Jamison woke up to Vivian in our room, sitting on my bed.

Please don't be her, I think to myself while holding my breath. She can't help it, I tell myself. She just loves me too much. Another door opens in the hallway and I hear my brother's angry voice.

"What are you doing?"

I hear my mother whisper, but I can't make out what she says. My brother is angry and his voice gets louder. "We had a deal. You are supposed to stay away from him."

I carefully make my way out of bed and creep towards my door in time to see Vivian's silk nightgown disappear across the hall into my brother's room.

Does he know what's been happening? She told me it was just me. I slide down my bedroom wall before planting myself against it on the floor. I wipe my wet eyes with the back of my hands before sending out a silent prayer. One day, we will get out of here and when we do, we won't ever look back.

Chapter 4

Jamison

Seventeen years old

"You guys are lucky to be alive." the officer states. "Had you heard the intruders and tried to help your parents, they might have killed you both."

"Where are our parents?" Jonathan asks from next to me.

"I'm sorry, but they didn't make it," another woman answers, as she walks up next to the officer and stares down at us both. She looks important, with her business suit and her fancy badge. *'The type of woman who probably gets off on touching little boys,'* I think, sneering to myself. The last memory I had with our adoptive parents crashes into me.

"You boys will age out soon. That's when you get to have real fun. After all, you put your time in," my foster father says with a smile. My brother, Jonathan, says nothing as he sits at the dinner table next to me. "We will have to make another appearance tomorrow night, though."

"You said last time was the last time," I grit out. My fingers dig into the sides of my chair as I fight to control my anger. I so badly want to reach across the table and wrap my hands around his neck. I want to watch his life fade from his eyes as I strangle him with my bare hands. My brother sits stiff beside me, probably thinking my same thoughts. We've both grown so much in the past year, both in height and weight. We've been working out and training in multiple forms of combat. Our parents don't know it yet, but we won't be making any appearances at The Cellar ever again.

My father narrows his eyes at me. "It's been almost a year,

Jamison. You know the rules. Multiple visits a year until fourteen. Once a year until eighteen. And if you cause a problem like last year, I'll make sure Jonathan takes your visit as well."

"I only gave her what she asked for," I growl out. Inside, the memory of Mrs. Palmer screaming as I held her down and fucked her until she bled surfaces. It took three guards to pull me off of her that night, and after, she had me strapped down so she could perform her own sick punishments on me. Everything she did to me that night was worth it when I got to watch her limp around in pain from my assault. She'd told me over the years how much she loved my fire while she abused me. It was only fair I finally got to show her. She was marked on my list the first time she put her disgusting hands on my body and one day, I truly would get the chance to pay her back.

"She couldn't leave her house for a week," my mother exclaims. She's acting like she gives a fuck about anything other than herself. She's just as bad as that bitch and she's just as sick. They all are.

"There won't be an issue," my father says sternly.

I nod my head in agreement but don't say a word.

"Your mother and I will retire for bed. You both should get some sleep as well." Without another word, they both excuse themselves and exit through to their wing of the house.

An hour later, both Jonathan and I sneak through their hall, gasoline and rope in hand. The grunts and moans sound through their door as we approach their bedroom. My father is the first to see Jonathan as we enter. He stops mid thrust as he stares at him, rope dangling from Jonathan's fingers.

"Well, this is new." He laughs. He's on his knees with our mother bent over doggy style. She peers sideways, trying to get a better look at what is happening. "Did you come to play? I know how much your mother would enjoy your baby cock."

"How about you choke on it instead?" I sneer as I come up behind him and wrap the rope in my hands around his neck. He immediately starts flailing around, attempting to pull the rope from his neck, but my grip is too tight. Our mother screams and tries to push herself from the bed, but Jonathan is on her immediately. He wraps the ropes around her wrists intricately behind her back before doing the same with her ankles.

"Beautiful," I muse. Our father grows slack in my arms as he passes out from his lack of oxygen. I drop him to the bed and tie him up as well. Jonathan looks at me with his signature smile while we both enjoy our work.

"Jon..Jonathan? Baby, what are you doing?" Our mother stutters out, making my brother's brows crease. The small sign of remorse flicks across his face, making me growl out.

"Don't fucking talk to him." I can see the turmoil consuming him. I suffer from lack of emotion while my brother is the complete opposite. My better half, essentially.

"They won't hurt us ever again, brother," I say, grabbing his chin and forcing him to look at me.

She cries out from the bed, "But I love you."

"You don't fucking love him!" I scream at her as I grab the gas can and start to pour it over her body. "You need him for your sick pleasure."

She sputters, as I pour it over her face, and continues to cry uncontrollably. Next, I pour it over my father. He wakes as the gasoline hits him, crying out in alarm.

"What the fu–," he starts, looking at me. "Boys? What do you think you are doing?"

"What we should have done a long time ago, father." I reply. Jonathan pulls out the lighter in his pocket and flicks it open. Our mother screams out in surprise when she realizes what is about to happen.

"Allow me," I say, closing my hand around my twin's wrist, noting his hesitancy. His bright blue eyes meet my dark ones.

"Don't you fucking dare!" our father screams from the bed, while rolling around in an attempt to escape.

"I need to do this," Jonathan says. His eyes never leave mine as he tosses the lighter onto the bed and it erupts in flames beside us. The sound of our parents screaming assaults us immediately. We don't stay to watch. We can't take the chance, so we quickly make our way back to our wing of the house.

"Jamison?" The woman questions, ripping me from my memory. "Are you sure you guys didn't hear anything?" She's looking at us both skeptically.

"Nothing," I reply. "We never hear anything on that side of the house." The woman nods her head before writing a few things down on her clipboard and walking away. I watch as she walks over to another officer and they both speak in hushed tones.

"Do you think they suspect anything?" Jonathan asks me, worry in his tone.

"It doesn't matter," I reply. "They won't be able to prove anything. It was set up to look like a break in and everyone who's anyone knows our parents might have made a few enemies in their lifetime."

"What do you think will happen now?"

I stare at the burnt walls on the side of the house as I pull a pack of cigarettes from my back pocket. "The lawyers will take care of helping with the estate." I say as I light a cigarette and inhale. "Normally, we would be sent to stay with someone else, but since we are almost eighteen, there won't be a need. Whoever is in charge of the estate will take over until then. It's only a few months away. After that, everything is ours."

I feel Jonathan's hand grab mine and squeeze. "So, it's over?"

"They won't ever touch us again, brother. From now on, it's just you and me, and no one will ever hurt us again," I reply, squeezing his hand back.

Chapter 5

Kaz

Seventeen years old

"No, no, no...where is it?" I mutter to myself while searching my closet for the third time. There is no sign of the zipper pouch containing the money I have been saving up for the past year anywhere. I don't know why I am still looking. I know exactly where it was—safely shoved in an old shoebox behind a small pile of clothes in the back of my tiny makeshift closet. The shoebox was there when I came home, closed up tight.

I knew the minute I walked into my room that something was wrong. I slump down against my closet wall and wipe the lone tear that slides down my cheek. All of my savings just... gone. I can't escape this hellhole if I can't pay for college. That was enough money to get me through at least the first year. I planned on earning the rest each summer in between.

"Charisma, baby, where are you? Can you bring me some water?" I hear my mother yell groggily through the paper-thin wall of our trailer. I walk out of my door and turn into her room to see her slumped over the side of her bed like she dropped something on the floor. Her hair is a matted mess, and the dingy nightshirt she is wearing has burn holes scattered across it.

"Jesus, Mother," I say, rushing in and lifting her body up to sit against the wall. Track marks cover her arm, making me grimace. My foot kicks something on the ground, and I lean down to pick up the lighter she must have dropped.

"Were you in my room, Mother? Did you go through my things?"

"I have no idea what you are talking about," she mumbles incoherently, with her eyes closed. No doubt, nodding off again. How convenient, I think to myself as I roll my eyes. She doesn't notice as I pocket her lighter and leave the room to head to our small kitchen and fill her a glass of water. The screen door slams, causing me to jump, and I spin around quickly. Pete, my mother's dealer boyfriend, waltzes in like he owns the place before leaning against the wall and crossing his arms. He stares at me, wetting his lips with his tongue.

"She's in her room," I say, gesturing to her doorway before turning around and putting the glass on the countertop. I close my eyes and try to conjure up any image in my head to erase Pete's disgusting face from my mind. A body pushes against me from behind, making my stomach roll. Pete puts both hands on the counter, caging me in.

"You're filling out more and more every day, Kaz. When you gonna let me tap this?" He grinds his dick against my ass, making me cringe. I spin around attempting to push him back, but he is much bigger and stronger than me. He cages me in further, causing me to lean back over the counter.

"Never gonna happen," I grit out.

He laughs in my face, showing off his yellow teeth.

"Never say never, sweetness. Your mama likes this dick. Hell, every other drug whore in this trailer park likes this dick. It's only a matter of time before you'll be down on your knees begging for a bag of rocks, too."

I push him again, and he steps back this time. Grabbing the glass of water from the counter, I shove it into his hand.

"I'm not a whore, and I'm never gonna come begging for drugs."

I hear his laugh follow behind me as I grab my hoodie off the couch and escape out the front door. The sound of the screen slams behind me, and I throw my hood over my head as I jog across the dead lawn and onto the small road. I can still hear Pete laughing as I make my way out of the trailer park. Fucking disgusting asshole. I'm a block down the road when a beat-up

Ford F-150 pulls next to me. A smile forms on my face when I see my best friend, Ben, in the driver's seat.

"Hey, sweet cheeks, you need a ride?" he asks in his most obnoxious, trucker voice.

I visibly cringe, making him laugh out loud before opening the passenger door and hopping in. "This is nice," I say, running my fingers across the dash. "Whose is it?"

"Mine," he replies with a smile. "It ain't a Jag, but I guess it'll do."

Now it's my turn to laugh. "Anything is nice when you don't have a car, Ben."

"True. Why haven't you used your money to get a car yet?"

He's not wrong in asking. My eyes linger on the corded muscles in his arm as he drives the truck. I don't know when, but at some point, my best friend went from boy to man.

"Stop checking me out and answer my question, Kaz." he laughs. "You know I don't play for your team."

"I know, I know, but if you did…"

"It would be you," he smirks while finishing my sentence.

I lean back in the chair and sigh. "You know I was saving it for college. I can't rely on underground fighting forever. I want to get out of here. I need to get away."

He nods his head in agreement. "I get it, and I don't blame you. You're right; you can't fight forever. Plus, your hacking skills are subpar at best, so we know you won't be making money off that unless you plan to sell fake IDs forever," he jokes.

I shove him in the arm and turn on the radio. One year ago, Ben introduced me to a few people who ran an underground fighting ring. He didn't want to, but I begged him one day when he showed up at my house with bruised ribs, a black eye, and a wad of cash. I started training with them the next day and was ready for my first fight within six months. There aren't many girls who fight in the underground, so I had been against a guy who was thankfully in my weight class. I won my first fight thanks to his cocky attitude and slow right hook. After that, the fighting became addictive. The money was even more addictive.

I know I can't risk fighting like that once I'm in college full-time. Out here, it isn't unusual for trailer trash to sport bruises and split lips. I could never walk around like that in the city, at least not if I wanted to be a lawyer someday.

The music shuts off, pulling me from my thoughts. "What's going on, Kaz?" Ben asks me. "You okay?"

I blow out a breath before answering. "All my money is gone."

"What?" Ben asks. "Do you think it was Pete or your mom?"

I scrunch my eyebrows up. I didn't even think about Pete taking it. Shaking my head, I sigh. "No, I'm pretty sure it was my mother. I don't think Pete would take the time to look through my stuff like that."

"Fuck, I'm sorry. What are you gonna do?"

"I think I might have to defer college for a year. See if I can save up enough money to take some extra classes to make up the difference," I respond sadly.

"What if I told you I could hack the system? What if you start taking prerequisites now at a cheaper college, and once you have those under your belt, I can hack in and add you to the system of a more prestigious college? It would help you get hired at a big corporate law firm, and you could work your way up once you're in the door."

My eyes go wide. "You could actually do that?"

"I can do a lot of shit now, Kaz. I'll even teach you some more stuff over the next couple of years just in case you need that skill set when you're a big wig in New York City," he says laughing as he pulls his truck into the little diner his parents run. It turns out that I would need those skills more than I had ever imagined.

Chapter 6

Kaz

Twenty-two years old

"What am I going to do without you?" Lydia whines as she grabs the tray of shots I just poured. I roll my eyes at her and laugh.

"We literally live together. You're still going to see me every day."

She sighs out loud. "Ya until you decide you want to hang out with all the rich lawyers you work for. Won't be long before a sugar daddy comes along and snatches you up. Before you know it, you will be living in his penthouse suite and wiping your ass with one hundred-dollar bills."

"Okay, calm down. This isn't *Pretty Woman*." I pour a shot of vodka and slide it towards her. "My job description is HR. It's nothing to write home about. I doubt anyone is going to want to take home the Human Resources lady. Also, how dare you think I would shit on a one hundred-dollar bill." I reply with my hand on my hip. She giggles before taking her shot while holding her tray in her other hand. She walks away, sashaying her hips back and forth as she goes. I wipe down the bar top and start cleaning up a couple of glasses customers have left. I'm going to miss this when I start work at Bolt Corporation on Monday. I contemplated bartending on the weekends for the extra money, but I'm not sure I can swing that if I decide to start taking classes again. To the world, I already have a bachelor's in business administration. Nobody knows I have barely completed my third year except my best friend, Ben, from back home. While I didn't defer for a year, I did have to take fewer classes to keep up with bills and life in general. I feel a whirlwind of emotions stir inside. It's been a couple weeks since I've spoken to him and we never go that long between calls. I make a mental note to call him this week to catch up.

A piece of hair falls in my face and I brush it back behind my ear while I lean over, attempting to grab another glass off the bar top. My senses prickle, causing me to look up. My gaze connects with a set of bright blue eyes from across the bar. *'Holy hell,'* I think as I peruse the fine specimen who is currently sitting on a barstool with a few other guys who are bantering back and forth. He is leaning casually against the back of the stool with one leg up slightly on the footrest. The other leg is stretched out with his foot on the ground. He's got his elbow on the table and his jaw resting on his fist, just watching me. His brown hair with a slight curl hangs just above his eyes. His entire demeanor is screaming dangerous. A crisp white T-shirt and pressed jeans, I'm sure are worth more than my car, finish his look. He's even got a tattoo peeking out from under his sleeve. Yummy. If I could choose my type, this man would be it. Am I fucking drooling right now? Yes, yes I am. He smirks at me and my eyes widen before I look away quickly. I totally just got caught checking that man out. I suddenly feel insecure as I turn away from the bar and pretend to organize the liquor behind me. Why was he staring at me? I look down at my ripped jeans and black crop top, searching for a stain. When I see nothing, I whip out a small compact from my clutch and proceed to search my face for any imperfections. Running mascara, smudged lipstick, a huge zit? Nope, nothing. I roll my eyes at myself before slipping the compact back where it belongs. The guy was probably trying to get my attention for a drink or something and I'm over here ogling him like he's a fucking zoo animal. Get it together Kaz, you can't make tips if you scare away all the customers. I was trying not to drink on the job tonight since I like to make very bad decisions when alcohol is involved, but clearly, I'm in need of a warmup. I grab a bottle of whiskey and pour a quick shot. The glass hits the tip of my lips as I turn to face the bar and I freeze. Bright blue eyes burn into mine.

"Any chance you can make me one?" his voice comes out smooth as he leans against the bar. I look up at him and try to gauge his height. He's got to be at least 6'3. He's long and lean, but I can see the way his muscles strain against his shirt. Jesus, he would destroy me. My pussy flutters at that thought. Down, girl.

"I'm sorry what?" I ask him as I shake myself out of my stupor.

He smiles, putting his pearly white teeth on display, and leans over the bar.

"Any chance you can make me a shot too, Pretty Girl?"

"A shot? Oh, umm sure," I stutter out as I set my full shot down without drinking it. "What are you drinking tonight?"

"Whatever you're having," he replies, eyeing my drink.

'*Shit*', I think to myself. I'm really not supposed to drink with the customers. I look around the bar. Fuck it. The boss is off tonight anyway and Lydia is closing down with me. It will be fine.

"Jameson okay?" I ask him.

His eyes flash for a second, and he chuckles to himself before responding. "That sounds great."

I pour his shot and slide it towards him while grabbing mine.

"Thanks, Pretty Girl," he says as he clinks his glass against mine and we both down our shots. He slides a fifty dollar bill towards me. "Keep the change." His friends call over to him, causing him to nod his head at me before making his way back over to their table. I watch him walk away before looking around and realizing how busy the bar has gotten tonight. Lydia comes over to the bar with another order.

"Holy shit, it just got busy in here," she follows my gaze over to the table I'm staring at and smiles. "They are fucking delicious, huh?"

"Who are they?" I ask her, looking away quickly so he

doesn't catch me staring again.

"No clue." She shrugs. "Whoever they are, they have money. I've made two hundred dollars off that table already in tips. I hope they stay all night." She pushes the tray towards me. "Another round. Make them strong."

I laugh at her. "Are you trying to get them completely wasted so they keep tipping?"

"Fuck, Kaz. I'm hoping they are so wasted, they decide to take me home and move me in with them."

We both giggle at that admission. She's not wrong. They all look like they are made of money and dipped in gold. They definitely don't look like they belong in our shitty little dive bar, that's for sure. I look over before looking away when I catch him staring at me again. I'm usually not nervous, but the way he keeps staring at me like he might devour me is making me weak in the knees.

A few too many shots and a couple hours later, Lydia comes up to the bar with her tray and slides a napkin towards me.

"What's this?" I ask as she stares at it with a wide smile.

"Your sexy admirer over there asked me to give it to you."

I look over her shoulder and catch him staring again while his finger runs around the edge of his drinking glass.

"Earth to Kaz," she says, snapping her fingers in my face. "Open it before I die of anticipation."

I unwrap the napkin and stare at the four words written. *Come home with me*. I don't know whether to be excited that this perfect god of a man wants me or annoyed that he has the audacity to assume I will just go home with anyone from the bar. I crumple the napkin and toss it into the trash.

"I think you should do it," Lydia says giddily. "When was the last time you got laid anyway, Kaz? Please don't tell me it was Kevin. It's been like seven months."

"Actually nine, but who's counting?" I laugh out loud.

"Fuck, you're practically a virgin again!" She screams, causing me to cover her mouth with my hand. Thankfully, the bar is busy and the music is loud, so nobody hears. I take another shot as she stares at me, waiting for my answer. The warmth spreads down into my belly, turning hot as lava when I connect my eyes with his again.

"Fuck it," I say to her as I nod my head yes towards him. "I'm probably never going to see him again, anyway. What's one night of hopefully phenomenal sex?"

Lydia squeals before clapping her hands together. "I already have your location. If he gets crazy and gives serial killer vibes, just send me an SOS and I'll send the police. I require every single detail in the morning!"

I wrinkle my nose at her. "If he's a serial killer, I'll be dead before the cops get there, Lydia. But I appreciate the sentiment." She laughs before walking away.

'If he knows what's good for him,' I think to myself, *'he won't try to slice me into pieces tonight.'*

Chapter 7

Jonathan
Twenty-six years old

"You stare any harder and that chick is going to run the other way," Kane says, shoving my shoulder as I gaze over at the sexy little blonde behind the bar. Her hair is up in a messy bun and she's got on a casual pair of ripped jeans paired with a crop top. She is definitely dressed down. I bet she doesn't even realize how fucking sexy she is. I groan internally as I imagine her plump pink lips and emerald green eyes staring up at me. I watch her as she reaches up for another bottle of liquor. Her shirt lifts, showing off the intricate design of a back tattoo. It looks big. I wonder how far up it goes?

"Are you kidding me?" Liam says as he grabs me from the side and pinches my cheek. "Have you seen this guy? He's so damn good looking, a straight guy would probably suck him off!" Kane and Liam both laugh when I shove him off of me and all three of us stare at the blonde behind the bar.

"She's hot. Kind of has that dirty, girl next door vibe." Liam comments.

"What the fuck is that?" I ask, chuckling.

"You know. She looks innocent, like the girl next door, but that tattoo on her back screams I will get down on my knees and suck your soul through your dick."

I roll my eyes at him.

"He's not wrong," Kane murmurs. "She's definitely not who you would bring home to mom and dad."

I turn to both of them with a straight face. "It's a good

thing I don't have either of those, ya?" They both stare at me with wide eyes, realizing the joke they made in poor taste. I crack a huge smile at both of them and push out a laugh.

"Calm down, guys. I know you were just kidding around. No harm, no foul."

They both laugh uneasily before Chris comes over to our side and starts making crude jokes about a couple on the other side of the bar. *'We definitely don't belong here,'* I think as I look around. This is not a scene for my ivy league buddies, but I needed a different atmosphere tonight. Somewhere where we could chill out without business associates cornering me every two seconds. The law firm I help run is still fresh. Just two years in and we have already skyrocketed to the top in New York City. My good friend Sebastian is the CEO of Bolt Corporation. Between him, Xavier, Andre, my twin Jamison and I, we all run different parts of the firm. Normally, I would be out with them on a Saturday night, but Sebastian and Xavier are both out of town for the weekend visiting Andre. Jamison had something 'too important' to do that kept him locked in his room all day, so here I am hanging out in a dive bar, hoping the sexy little bartender takes me up on my offer. She looks over in my direction and nods a yes before turning towards her friend. I see her friend clap her hands together in excitement. Maybe I should ask her friend to come back with us? That might get Jamison to come out of his room. Who am I kidding? I would have better luck offering to share the bartender. I lick my lips, imagining that scene in my head. The pretty bartender on her hands and knees sucking my cock while she takes my brother from behind. I groan internally and adjust myself. I love fucking girls with Jamison. It's always better when they take us both.

A few hours go by of me watching her and the bar finally starts to clear out. My friends all leave, giving me high fives on their way out, as I saunter over to where she's at. I slide onto a stool at the bar and watch her as she cleans up some glasses. She looks at me nervously before looking away towards her waitress friend across the room.

"Change your mind? Afraid I'll kidnap you and hold you in a basement somewhere?" I ask, grinning.

A look of determination crosses her face and I see the fear in her eyes dissipate.

"You could try," she states so plainly, I would swear I was speaking to a whole different person if I didn't know any better. Fuck, that's sexy. This innocent little thing is suddenly so ballsy.

I smirk at her before raking my eyes down her body, memorizing every curve.

"I never caught your name, Pretty Girl."

She leans over the bar top towards me and the cut of her shirt drops, showcasing her cleavage and the peak of a lacy black bra.

"I think Pretty Girl is a good enough name for tonight, don't you?"

I'm suddenly caught a little off guard. Women usually throw themselves at me, immediately wanting to tell me every little detail about them. Those same women are also the ones I can't get to stop texting or calling me the day after we fuck. I'm not used to someone who isn't as privy to give out her information. I'm not sure how I feel about the situation. I quickly school my features and smile at her.

"Pretty Girl it is." I state before motioning for her to follow me. "Let's get out of here."

She grabs her friend and a few other workers leave as she locks up the bar.

"I have her location and if I don't get a text from her in the next few hours, I'll send the police. You got it, Buddy?" her friend yells across the parking lot as we walk to my bike.

"Got it," I holler back at her friend and laugh. "Guess I forgot to ask you if you're okay with getting on the back of my bike?" I ask, eyeing her.

She grins up at me as she responds, "I think I'm up for the ride."

My dick immediately jumps in my pants as I catch on to her double innuendo. I watch her bite her lip as I attach my helmet on top of her head. All I can think about is how I can't wait to bite it myself. I get on my bike and she hops on behind me, her tits pressing against my back as she wraps her arms around me and we take off.

Thirty minutes later, we pull up to my building and into the underground parking lot below it. As soon as I've removed the helmet off of her head, I lean over and kiss her. It's intoxicating, the way her mouth immediately opens for me. Her tongue swirls around mine and she nips my lip with her teeth before pulling back.

"I've been waiting to do that all night," I say to her with a grin as I lift her off the back and set her on the ground. "Come on."

I grab her hand, and she follows me into the elevator. I press her against the wall as the doors close behind us. She looks hesitant for a minute.

"You can still say no," I murmur as I kiss up her neck. She moans in my ear and grabs the back of my arms, pulling me closer.

"I'm not saying no," she whispers as she presses her body against mine. No doubt, she can feel my dick hard as a rock, right through my pants.

We pull apart as the doors open right into my suite, and I watch her eyes widen. "I'll give you a grand tour, but first, let's start with my bedroom," I say as I drag her to my room, shut the door and press her up against it.

She pushes me back a bit and suddenly I'm afraid she is really going to change her mind. I could have any girl over here in ten minutes flat if I wanted to, but there's something about Miss Bartender. I need to be inside her. I need to feel her body against mine, and fuck, I can't wait to hear her moans.

"Actually, I know this is going to sound crazy, but any chance I can use your shower first? I've been working all night and I'm kind of a hygiene freak."

Her request catches me a little off guard. "Yeah, of course you can. Just head right through that door over there. Mind if I join you in a few minutes?" I ask as I nip her bottom lip.

"I wouldn't be opposed to you washing my back for me." She smirks as she heads towards my en suite bathroom.

I groan as I watch her disappear before heading out of my bedroom and across the living room to my brother's room. I open his door without knocking to find him sitting at his desk. A pair of glasses sit on his nose as he types away on his computer without looking up.

"There's a hot blonde currently naked in my shower," I say as I lean against his door frame. "You want me to see if she's up for a tag team?"

"No," he says, still typing. He's been holed up with his computer since yesterday and it's really starting to irritate me. I walk over to the desk and lean against it, completely in his space.

"What is so important that you would turn down tits and ass, Jamison?"

He looks up at me, clearly annoyed, before dragging both hands down his face. I raise an eyebrow, still waiting for his response.

"Sebastian and Xavier hired someone new to head our Human Resources."

"Okay, and?" I ask him, perplexed.

He looks at me dead in the face before responding, "a woman."

I whistle before letting out a laugh. "I call first dibs. Maybe she will let me fuck her over her desk?" I say, resting my hand under my chin like I'm in deep thought.

"He failed to tell me about this new hire so I could run the proper background checks. I've been searching all day, but something does not add up with her credentials. I need more time."

"Maybe we can both fuck her over her desk at the same time?" I say, earning a glare from him. I sigh out loud because I know Jamison will likely be searching for the next decade if he doesn't get the answers he wants. "She's a woman, brother. How dangerous could she really be?"

"She starts Monday," he states as he leans forward and resumes his search. He is obviously dismissing me, but whatever.

"If you change your mind, I'll be across the way with a hot little bartender," I say as I exit his room. He doesn't bother responding as I shut his door and make my way back to my room. The door to my bathroom is slightly ajar and I can see steam seeping through the cracks. I remove my clothes as I go, not bothering to knock as I make my way into the bathroom. Fog permeates the bathroom, but not enough to shield my vision from the sexy woman currently humming in my shower as she washes her hair under the water. I have been with many women in my time, but this little blonde is the hottest fucking thing I have ever seen. She's tiny, with curves in all the right places. I hope I don't break her because something tells me one round with her won't be enough. I can see the entire intricate design of her tattoo that spans from the top of her spine all the way down before stopping right above her ass crack as I open the shower door to step in. She turns around quickly with wide eyes, giving me a full frontal view.

"Fuck me," I groan out loud when I see the sparkle of her nipple piercings. She bites her lip shyly before her eyes rake over my body and widen even further at the very large appendage currently standing at attention between my legs. I am not a small man in any way, shape or form, so I silently pray that she doesn't go running for the hills.

"Is that?" she asks, eyeing my dick.

"A Prince Albert? Yes." I say, cutting her off before pressing her up against the shower wall. My dick is so hard I might burst if I don't give it some sort of relief soon. I drop to my knees and hoist her up against the wall with both legs over my shoulders and her pussy directly in my face. Wasting no time, I lick right up the center of her slit, earning an "oh" as she grabs my head with one hand and attempts to hold the wall with the other. She tastes fucking divine.

I look up at her with a cocky as fuck smirk and we both

lock eyes.

"Forgive me, father, for I am about to sin," I say before diving in. She moans and pushes my head against her before rocking her ass back against the wall and my face. She has absolutely zero shame as she takes her pleasure and I am fucking here for it. At this point, I'm not even sure if I'm fucking her with my tongue or if she is fucking my tongue with her pussy. I use two of my fingers to glide into her tight little hole while I suck her clit into my mouth, earning another moan.

"Fuck, don't stop," she moans, pulling my head and hair so tightly against her pussy, I'm practically suffocating. If I go out like this, write that shit on my fucking grave. *Jonathan died doing what he loved.* I pump my fingers faster inside her and feel her clench around me before she screaming that she's coming. I don't stop licking until she's pushing my head away from her sensitive clit. She doesn't waste any time dropping to her knees and taking my length into her warm, wet mouth. She swallows me down and I feel my dick hit the back of her throat before she slides it back out again and looks up at me.

"Fuck, Pretty Girl. Who taught you to suck dick like that?"

"My gay best friend," she says, smiling.

I let out a surprised laugh. "Every girl needs one of those. Show me that again."

She licks up the side of my dick and cups my balls in one hand before squeezing my shaft with the other. Then she glides my dick right back into her mouth and lets it hit the back of her throat again. I thread my fingers through her wet strands and she lets me guide her head back and forth on my dick. I'm torn between wanting to fuck her face or her pussy, but if she keeps going like this, I might explode far quicker than I want to. I pull her off my dick and reach down to pick her up and throw her over my shoulder. She squeals and I smack her ass, exiting my shower and dripping water all over the floor. I don't care.

"I need to be inside you, Pretty Girl. I can't wait any longer," I say, dropping her wet body onto my bed, causing her tits to bounce. She smiles up at me as I yank both her legs and drag her down to the edge of my bed.

"You can still say no," I say as I open the drawer to my nightstand, unwrap a condom, and roll it onto my dick.

"No," she says with wide eyes, causing me to pause. No one's ever said no to me before and I'm all about consent. My hand is going to be so sore tomorrow because I swear I'm going to be up all night beating my dick to the memory of this sexy as fuck woman. Fuck.

She laughs when she sees the look of worry on my face. "Just kidding."

Sweet baby Jesus. I swear my dick weeps for joy when it hears that statement.

"Oh, Pretty Girl, you're going to regret that joke," I say as I grab her ass and drag her onto my dick in one swift motion.

"Fuck," she yells out. "You're so fucking big."

"You can take it, baby. You're doing so good." I praise her as I pump in and out.

She grabs the edge of the bed with both hands and uses it to push herself back and forth. The motion feels incredible as we both come apart and slam back together. I rub her clit with my thumb while I continue to fuck her.

"Fuck, you're such a good girl. Look at you fucking this big dick with your tight little pussy."

Her pussy spasms and she arches up, giving me an even better angle. My dick hits so deep I can feel her tighten clear up my shaft.

"Fuck! I'm coming," she screams out. The sound of her sexy moans send me spiraling. My balls draw up and I explode inside her with a roar, practically blacking out. Fuck, that was quick.

"I swear, I don't usually come that quick. Give me five minutes because I'm not even close to being done with you yet," I tell her as I remove the condom and toss it in the trash.

"I guess I could be persuaded," she says with a smirk as she stretches out across my bed. She really is beautiful. Smooth skin and perfect curves. Innocent looking with this wild side hidden beneath her clothes. My phone rings, pulling me out of my trance. It's Sebastian, and he rarely calls this late.

"I have to take this real quick," I say to her as I pull on a pair of sweatpants and exit onto my balcony. I slide the door shut before pressing the answer button on my phone and switching to the speaker.

"Is there a reason you're interrupting me while I have a beautiful woman naked on my bed right now?" I ask him sarcastically.

"I'm sure Jamison is keeping her occupied," he says with a laugh. I glance into my room and watch her disappear into my bathroom. I don't bother telling him Jamison is on an all night binger because of the new employee he decided to hire, and most certainly won't be joining me. The thought doesn't even bother me, which is weird. The sex I just had with Miss Bartender was fucking phenomenal. I can't wait to rub it in his face tomorrow.

Sebastian's voice cut through the line. "Earth to Jonathan. Listen, I'm going to let you get back to your hot piece of ass. You know I don't sleep well. I was just going over some information with one of our cases and wanted to pick someone's brain. Xavier didn't answer so I'll probably hit up Andre."

I laugh. "You really need to get a hobby, Sebastian. I'll call you tomorrow."

He grunts before hanging up. I slide the door back open and enter the room, looking around. She's not in the bedroom, so I make my way over to the bathroom door that is currently wide open. I peek my head in, noticing she isn't in there either. Maybe she got hungry and went looking for food?

"Did you want me to order something to eat, Pretty Girl?" I ask out loud while entering my living room. It's quiet, and I don't see her anywhere. My brows scrunch up. Where the fuck did she go? I slam Jamison's door open and find him sitting in the exact same spot he was when I last entered.

"Hey, you hiding a blonde in here? About five foot nothing, long blonde hair, curvy with nice perky tits?"

"No." he states, his eyes glued to the screen.

"Whatever," I respond, before slamming his door closed. "I didn't need you tonight, anyway." I mutter to myself. The memory of the sexy bartender wriggling beneath me while I pound into her flashes through my brain while I flop onto my damp bedsheets. Fuck, I didn't even catch her name or her number. Normally, I wouldn't give a fuck, but there's something about her I can't put my finger on. It was good. Fuck, it was better than good. Suddenly, I find myself tired. I fall asleep thinking about all the things I plan on doing to her the next time I see her. But first, I'll need to hit up that dingy little dive bar again so I can get her information.

Chapter 8

Jamison
Twenty-six years old

I rub the sleep from my eyes as I make my way into Bolt Corporation, Monday morning. I didn't sleep all weekend. Between digging up intel on the new employee Sebastian hired and jerking off to the memory of hearing my brother fuck whoever was in his room Saturday night, I've barely slept. I don't do jealousy, but I'll admit, my brother never has that much fun unless we fuck someone together. If the little slut wouldn't have run out on him when she did, I probably would have taken him up on his earlier offer. I was two seconds from barging into his room and choking her with my cock just to shut her up. I groan and hit the elevator button. Three days of digging and I have finally found the information I needed. I tried to call Sebastian earlier this morning, but he didn't answer. Hopefully, I can get to his office before he decides to give this new woman the grand tour. The elevator dings and I press down on the cuffs of my suit, smoothing the creases around my wrists. I enter before turning around and watch as the elevator doors start to close.

"Wait," a feminine voice speaks as a dainty hand pushes against one of the doors. Light pink fingernails curve against the edge pressing into the metal. The motion sends an image of them wrapped around my dick. I don't make a move to help with the door. I'm too busy wondering which of our interns decided to paint their nails such a perfectly poised and innocent color. The doors finally take the hint and open back up, revealing the goddess behind them. Her pictures didn't do her justice. She is absolutely devastating. She's wearing an all black pin skirt that hugs her hips perfectly. Her crisp white blouse is pressed neatly. Not a professional pressing, but an adequate job nonetheless. She has on sleek black heels and her blonde hair is pulled back into a neat french twist. Her emerald green eyes widen when she sees me. I stare at her, emotionless, while my brain explodes inside. How dare she waltz in here, looking like that, and think she can just play our entire company.

"Umm, hello," she says nervously as she walks into the elevator and stands beside me. I don't look down at her, even though I can see her peeking at me from the corner of her eye. It doesn't matter. She won't be here long, anyway. The elevator begins its ascension while I stand beside her, silently stewing in my anger. Suddenly, she turns towards me.

"Aren't you going to say anything?"

"What would you like me to say?" I reply to her without looking her way.

She huffs. "I don't know. Anything…"

Anger floods through me and I can't help myself. Normally I am a master of keeping my emotions in check, but this woman has gotten under my skin already. I just met her, yet I feel like three days of combing the internet of every little detail concerning her has me coming unhinged. I turn towards her and slam my hand above her shoulder, caging her against the wall of the elevator. She shrinks away from me; the motion causing my dick to stir.

"If you think for one second you're going to just waltz in here and derail this company, you have another thing coming. I have spent every waking moment preparing us perfectly for the future. I won't have some inadequate woman coming in here and flipping over everything we have worked for." I slam my hand above her again to get my point across. She flinches before glaring up at me.

"What the hell is your problem?"

Her tone surprises me. She went from a timid little kitten to a raging kitty with her claws out in no time flat. If my dick wasn't hard before, it certainly is now.

"You. Are. My. Problem." I lean in close as I grit out the words.

Her features soften, and she places her hand on my suit in a calming gesture.

"Look, I'm sorry. I'm freaking out here, okay? I have this perfect job that landed in my lap and I don't want to screw it up. I really need this. You don't understand. Could we just start over?" She bites her lip and blinks a few times while looking away. Fuck, why do I feel so indecisive right now? I shouldn't be letting her fake show of tears affect me. It's not the company's problem. Before I can respond, the elevator doors ding, letting us know we have hit our floor. I quickly turn back, standing up and straighten my suit jacket. I don't care how beautiful this woman is or what sob story she gives. She is not staying.

"Don't get comfortable," I say without giving her another look before exiting the elevator and making my way to our meeting room. Sebastian, Andre and Jonathan are all already inside conversing.

"I have been trying to contact you all morning, Sebastian," I say as I pull my chair out and sit down.

"I was in the gym. Figured it could wait until work, no?"

I stare at him without responding.

He gets the message loud and clear before leaning back in his chair. "Okay, Jamison. Lay it on me."

Before I get the chance to start the conversation, the little devil herself makes an appearance with Xavier in tow.

"...and I promise, you are going to love it here. Don't believe the tabloids. The Men of Bolt Corporation are harmless," Xavier says, laughing. We all stand up and I glare at her. She looks at me and then looks over towards Jonathan and her eyes go wide. Surely this woman has seen twins before.

"Pretty Girl?" Jonathan asks. I look over at him quizzically before looking back at her. She stands there like a deer caught in headlights.

Xavier laughs, breaking the silence. "You two know each other?"

Suddenly, it all clicks together. My brother's incessant chatter all day yesterday about the sexy bartender he dubbed Pretty Girl because she wouldn't give him her name. He went as far as going back to the bar last night to try to find her again. He came home acting like a kicked puppy when they informed him that Saturday night had been her last night working there.

"We met a while back," Jonathan says nonchalantly when he realizes everyone is staring at him.

"Umm okay," Xavier says. "Everyone meet Charisma Fields. She is our new head of Human Resources."

"Thank you," she replies. "You can just call me Kaz." She looks over at Jonathan quickly as she says it before looking around the room to everyone else except me. She's avoiding eye contact. I look over at my brother, who practically has stars in his eyes. I've never seen him look this way and I don't like it. He doesn't need some woman coming into his life and turning it upside down.

"Okay, now that that is settled." Sebastian says as he rings in his assistant and tells her to come up to the meeting room and show Kaz to her new office. "What was it you wanted to discuss that was so important, Jamison?"

Kaz's eyes shoot towards me and she stares at me, silently pleading. My brother is still looking at her like she's air and he's drowning. Her pouty lips push out nervously and images of her wrapping them around my dick while Jonathan fucks her blow through my mind. Suddenly, I'm at a loss for words.

"It was not important. More research is needed before we speak further," I reply, not taking my eyes off of Kaz. I see her visibly relax before closing her eyes for a second and breathing out. Blakely, Sebastian's newest assistant, appears before guiding Kaz out the door. She looks at both my brother and I over her shoulder as she walks out and the door closes behind her.

"Head of HR is off limits, boys," Sebastian states, causing Andre to groan.

"Really Sebastian? You know I love blondes," Andre says, causing him and Xavier to laugh.

Jonathan's knuckles go white as he grips the chair beside me. I can feel his jealousy ripple through me, almost as if it were my own.

"Off. Limits." Sebastian says again. "The tabloids have been having a heyday with our company recently, and we're too new to be grabbing this kind of attention. I already had to pay off your last assistant, Andre. She threatened to sue us through our rival firm for your little charade you pulled last month."

"She wanted to suck me off. I didn't think she would care that I invited someone else to come in and help her out," Andre says laughing.

Sebastian sighs and rolls his eyes. He knows he's not much better when it comes to the women who work for us. They are all willing and eager to please, so what are we to do?

"Assistants are fair game. Fuck the rest of HR for all I care, but do not fuck Kaz. We need one woman here to last more than six months or we are going to go bankrupt paying them off before we make it big." He looks around the room before focusing directly on me and then on Jonathan. "Are we clear?" Jonathan nods.

"Crystal," I respond as my stomach turns.

This is going to be a fucking disaster.

Chapter 9

Kaz

Two years later

I step out of my shower and wrap a towel around my hair, securing it on top of my head. My cell vibrates on the countertop, showing multiple missed messages and a few calls. I swipe to the first set and bite my lip as I read them.

Hey, Pretty Girl...
I haven't seen you at work all week.
Are you avoiding me again? I can still taste you on my lips.

Fuck, why do his words get to me like this? It's been a few weeks since I texted Jonathan drunk off my ass asking for him to pick me up. He did without question and took me to the same ritzy hotel he has been for the past few years. From there, he proceeded to do the most ungodly things to my body all night long before passing out next to me in bed. I snuck out on him again per usual and then had to deal with the onslaught of his text messages the entire next day while I ignored them. I knew from the first time I slept with him at his apartment that we would never work. I remember looking around his room while I sat on his expensive Sferra bed sheets, thinking how out of place I was. Who the fuck even spends two grand on bedsheets, anyway? I was like a paper plate surrounded by fine china and completely out of my element. I never would have guessed I would be working for him until that next Monday when I had shown up to Bolt Corporation and ran into his asshole twin. His identical twin might I add.

Jamison is just as sexy as his brother, but he is a complete and utter asshole. He finds every opportunity to let me know I don't belong and makes sure to remind me just how grateful I should be that he is keeping my secret. He also constantly reminds me to stay away from Jonathan. If Jonathan was a dick like his brother, it would certainly make life much easier. The upside is, working for Bolt Corporation has increased my bank account substantially. The pay is incredible so I can't afford for to lose this job. Hence me attempting to stay off Jamison's radar and away from Jonathan. Alas, I'm feeling extra weak tonight and I've only had one drink just to relax. I need someone to talk me down from this ledge I'm about to jump off of. I scroll through my notifications and realize I have a couple of missed calls from my best friend, Ben. *'Just the person I can count on to catch me before I fall,'* I think, smiling as I click his contact to call him back. The phone rings and rings before going to voicemail.

"Hi friend," I say into the recorder. "I've only had one drink, but I need you right now. I'm feeling like I might decide to go impale myself on..." I look down at my phone screen when I hear the beep of an incoming call and see Ben's contact flash on my screen. I quickly switch calls.

"Bestie! Please stop me from being a pathetic little bitch tonight."

The line is silent for a minute.

"Ben?" I ask again as I look down at my screen to make sure the call is still connected.

I hear a sigh before a gruff voice comes up on the line.

"Hey Kaz, It's David, Ben's dad."

"Why do you have Ben's phone?" I ask, hesitantly.

"Listen, Ben's missing. We haven't seen or heard from him in four days. All his stuff was at his place. There was no sign of a struggle. The authorities said they can't do anything more and are closing the case."

"What? That doesn't make any sense. I just spoke to him a few days ago." I scroll through my call log before realizing our last conversation was six days ago.

"Do you know where he could have gone?" His dad asks me.

"No, I mean he wouldn't have just left like that," I respond. "Why didn't you guys call me sooner?" I ask, angrily

"The authorities tried to call you but you didn't answer. I've been a little busy looking for my son and consoling my wife," he bites back, making me cringe.

'Fuck,' I think to myself when I realize I have multiple voicemails I haven't checked all week. Work has been slammed and I haven't had a lot of time to catch up on personal stuff lately.

"I'm sorry. Will you please let me know if anything changes?"

David sighs. "Yeah, I will. But Kaz, I'm not stupid. I know what Ben was into. It was only a matter of time before everything caught up with him. I was kind of hoping he had run off to hide with you in New York."

I scrunch my eyes together in an attempt to hold off the tears. I don't think I can believe he would have run away without telling me. Something tells me, whatever happened to my best friend isn't good. The worst part is that there is not a damn thing I can do about it.

"Don't come here, Kaz," he says before hanging up.

"I won't," I respond out loud to myself. "Why wouldn't you tell me if something was going on, Ben?"

Fuck, I need an escape. I can't think right now. Tears blur my vision. I have to get out of here. Before I know what I'm doing, I'm throwing on a long maxi dress and putting my hair up in a bun. A few quick swipes of mascara and some lip gloss is the only effort I'm attempting to make before slipping out of my door.

I look up at the neon sign blinking before entering the shop. Janie drops her combat boots off the desk and drops the magazine she's currently reading.

"Kaz." she smiles, before running over and hugging me. "It's been a while, girl. Looking for some therapy tonight?"

"I was hoping to make an appointment. I know how busy

Tex gets." I respond, attempting to smile back. I'm fully aware I could have called, but I really needed to get out of my apartment and get some fresh air.

She grabs both my shoulders, eyeing me. "You okay, girl?"

I look away and hold back tears before looking back at her. "Ya, I just haven't been having the best day. How about that appointment, though?"

Janie gets the hint before letting me go and putting on her signature smile. "Sure thing. Tex is actually just finishing someone up right now and he had a cancellation afterwards. Depending on what you want, he might be able to fit you in."

We are interrupted by the sway of a curtain and Tex's face peaking through. "Well look what the cat drug in," he says as he walks out, removing his gloves. I catch a momentary glimpse of a completely inked torso with a very large surgical patch covering just below the navel. The abs on the unknown customer are insane. I'm momentarily stunned into silence before Tex draws the curtain back closed.

"Umm yeah, I was hoping to make an appointment." I say to him.

"What are you wanting done?"

"Well, I was hoping to add on to what we have been doing but I'll take anything at this point," I reply.

He looks at me quizzically like he is assessing me before turning to Janie. "Put her on my books for right now. I just finished up. I'm taking a quick smoke break out back. Prep for me." He turns and walks away and I catch Janie sticking her tongue out at him.

"He could at least say please." She scoffs as she heads to the desk to put me on the schedule. "Looks like your day is turning around after all, isn't it, Kaz? Kaz? Hey, are you sure you're okay?"

I look back at her to realize Janie's been talking and I've completely zoned out while looking out the front windows.

"I'm sorry, I didn't even hear you. I think I need a minute. Do you mind if I use the restroom real quick?"

Janie eyes me with concern before nodding her head. "Of course, girl. You know where it's at."

I head past a few empty stations with open curtains and pass the last closed curtain before turning into a small hall and open the bathroom door before gasping. A shirtless man stands facing away from me, hovering over the sink with his head down. His back is completely filled with ink. An entire ship scene covers it. The top clears the upper half of his back, starting with the ship and ending with a sky filled with crows that stop right about where the collar of a shirt would start. The underwater part covers the lower part of his back, disappearing beneath the waistband of his black slacks. There isn't one single portion untouched. I lick my lips subconsciously while wondering what could possibly be tattooed below. The muscles in his shoulders and back tense up and ripple making my insides squirm. Holy hell, this man is making me wet and I haven't even seen his face. There's only one other man with muscles rivaling these and he is a lot less tatted than this guy. Unfortunately, said man is completely off limits.

"Shit, I'm sorry," I say shaking myself out of my stupor and turning towards the door to leave. My hand pulls the handle and the door opens a few inches before a hand slams it closed above me. I close my eyes attempting not to freak the fuck out before a breathe whishpers into my ear.

"Hello Kitten," Jamison purrs in my ear. "Is there a reason you followed me here? Sick of my brother already?"

My entire body tenses up and I whip around angrily to face him.

"What the fuck are you talking about? I didn't follow you here. I have an appointment. And there's nothing going on with your brother so leave it alone already. You are the last person I would decide to follow." I put my hand up to his chest to push him away and realize my mistake immediately. I can feel his muscles ripple beneath my palm and fuck if it doesn't send a jolt right to my pussy. I look down, noting the ink sprawled across but I don't have time to assess anything before he grabs my hand

and slams it against the door above me.

"Do you think I'm a foolish man, Kitten? Do not insult my intelligence. I know everything that happens with my brother." He presses himself against me and I can feel the hard planes of his body brush up against the thin fabric of my dress. I let out a small whimper and he smirks down at me.

"We are identical. Do not pretend that you aren't attracted to me."

"I'm not," I grit out. "You are an asshole."

Before I know what's happening, Jamison has my dress hiked up above my hips. He pushes my thong aside before swiping two fingers across my very wet slit. I squeeze my eyes shut in embarrassment. He grips my jaw tightly with his other hand forcing my eyes to open. Two wet fingers glisten in front of me.

"Do tell me again all about how unattracted you are." He squeezes my jaw again, causing me to gasp in pain as he shoves both fingers into my mouth. "Taste those sweet lies, Kitten."

My mouth automatically closes around his fingers and I involuntarily suck. Before I can comprehend what is happening, Jamison has my leg up over his thigh and is plunging his other two fingers into my pussy. I lean my head back against the door and moan around the fingers he still has shoved into my mouth.

"Such a little slut you are," he growls in my ear. "You sneak around fucking my brother and letting me fingerfuck you in a tattoo parlor bathroom."

Fuck, why is this turning me on. I should be pissed off right now. I should be telling him to get the fuck away from me but the sound of his dirty words are destroying me. This isn't the perfectly poised and controlled Jamison I'm used to. This is an unhinged God and right now, I feel like a willing servant. My pussy tightens with every pump of his fingers.

"Do you feel how wet you are, Kitten? You're going to come for me like the dirty slut you are, aren't you?"

I try to shake my head no but he swipes his thumb across my clit while still plunging his fingers inside me and it sends me over the edge. I come with a muffled cry, his two fingers still shoved in my mouth while the others grip around my jaw. My leg drops to the ground suddenly along with my dress and I open my eyes to look into a set of glaring deep blue ones. Tears track down both sides of my face. Jamison leans in close.

"You are here because I allow it. Jonathan will tire of you and your antics one day. He will see you for what you are or I will show him." He lets me go suddenly before pulling the door open, causing me to stumble forward. Without another word, he's gone, and I'm left a complete and utter mess. My brain is in overdrive while my pussy is screaming for more. Holy fucking hell. What have I just gotten myself into?

Chapter 10

Jonathan
Three years later

Where are you? We are about to start the morning meeting. Your punctuality is nauseating.

I roll my eyes at the text from my twin as I enter the elevator and lean against the back in the corner. Kaz enters and quickly averts her eyes when she notices I'm also in there.

"Morning," I say, flashing her my dazzling smile as a few more people slide into the elevator. A curvy brunette enters with her nose wrinkled and stands next to Kaz.

"What's wrong," I hear Kaz whisper to the woman. "You don't like the smell of 'I have a small dick but I'm gonna act like it's big energy' either?" They both break out in a fit of giggles. Kaz turns her head towards me and the woman's gaze follows. I smirk at Kaz and she rolls her eyes. She is trying to goad me, I know it. What I really want to do is corner her in this damn elevator and slide my hand up her skirt. Pump my fingers into her tight little pussy and make her confess to everyone around about how she was just riding my dick over the weekend like I was a fucking racehorse. Nevermind the fact that she was drunk...again. She can pretend she doesn't want me all she wants, but we both know the truth. The only thing stopping me is the thought of someone else hearing her pretty little moans while she comes on my fingers. Well that, and the fact that the CEO, Sebastian, would gut me if he found out I was fucking the one person at Bolt Corporation he deemed off limits from day one. He is one of my best friends but his controlling nature is ridiculous. Right up there next to Jamison. I've had to resort to picking Kaz up everytime she calls me wasted and booking a hotel room just to avoid him finding out what I am up to. I'm honestly surprised he hasn't yet but I know he is suspicious. We do most everything together including sometimes sharing our conquests. Kaz isn't a conquest to me though. I don't want to share her with anyone. I also don't want to upset my brother so I'll remain a dirty little secret…for now. The elevator dings and I watch her walk out with the other woman. She doesn't so much as glance back in my direction but that's okay. I know it's just a matter of time before she calls me again.

Chapter 11

Kaz

A few months later

"Please say you'll meet up with me later," Jonathan whispers in my ear as he presses up against me. My whole body ignites with him this close and I involuntarily lean into him causing him to groan. "You're killing me, Kaz."

I glance around wildly, making sure we can't be seen. The curtain is purely for decoration and we are shoved into a corner behind it. Still, I can't relax knowing any minute we could be caught.

"Jonathan, please," I plead with him while he proceeds to kiss up my neck. "Someone is going to catch us. We can't keep doing this." I'm breathless and two point five seconds from hitching up my dress and letting him fuck me right here behind this curtain at our fucking company Christmas party. What the hell is wrong with me? Coming to my senses, I push against him, backing him up and peer around the corner. I see Riley come in with a man who looks completely wasted. I'm assuming it's her husband. Gross. That woman has no idea how amazing she is. Any man would be falling to their knees for a chance to be here with her…sober.

"Fuck, Riley's here," I turn to walk around the curtain but Jonathan grabs my hand and jolts me towards him, conveniently placing it on his dick.

"Look how hard you make me, Pretty Girl." He pushes his lips out into a pout and it causes his dimple to pop. I bite my lip while perusing his face and body. His hair is disheveled per usual sweeping across his forehead like he doesn't have a care in the world. The top two buttons of his suit are open and his tie is loose around his neck. He is so fucking sexy, it almost hurts to look at him. What's worse is he knows it. He smirks at me as he rubs my palm over his cock nonchalantly. I snatch my hand back once I realize what he's doing.

"Stop it. Fuck Jonathan, you are going to get us caught. I have to go." I turn and whip out from behind the curtain and strut right up to Riley, her very pissed off looking husband and a smug Sebastian.

"Oh my God, Riley, you look beautiful! I knew that dress was going to look stunning on you!" I can feel the tension thick in the air so I turn towards Nate and place my hand on his shoulder hoping to calm the situation. "You must be Nate. It's nice to meet you. You sure are a lucky man to have such a beautiful woman on your arm tonight!" He says nothing. Asshole. I grab Riley's hand and start dragging her away while Nate follows. "I need you to come over here so I can introduce you to a few people."

"Thank you," Riley whispers when Nate looks back towards Sebastian.

"I got you," I reply before we make our rounds around the room for introductions with other employees and acquaintances from Bolt Corp. I spend the next hour checking on employees and avoiding Jonathan. Everytime I look in his direction or get near him, I catch Jamison watching me like a hawk. He is way too observant for his own good. I've already had a few drinks and I'm definitely feeling tipsy. Tipsy enough to meet with Jonathan later...most likely.

I'm stuck in my thoughts zoning out on Jonathan when commotion from Riley's side of the table catches my attention. Nate pukes all over Sasha, causing me to grimace. I don't have time to fully comprehend the situation when I see Jamison's tall form stand up. His deep blue eyes blaze as he stalks towards me. His suit is crisp, completely buttoned and perfectly pressed. Not an ounce of ink showing. His hair styled back like he just came off the set of a GQ photoshoot. I gulp and spin around, frantically searching for an escape. I don't know why he looks so mad but I'm not sober enough to deal with him right now. I spot a server's door and quickly scoot through it before turning into a low lit hall. *'These must be offices,'* I think to myself as I try a few doors that are locked. Finally, a knob turns and I push myself into a room before silently closing it behind me. Definitely an office, but at least I can catch my breath for a minute while I'm in here. I don't dare turn the lights on. Plus, there's plenty of light shining through the open window that I can see perfectly fine, minus a few shadows, of course. I've just made my way to the desk when a voice speaks from behind me. I shriek and spin around quickly, my hand on my heart.

"Why are you running, Kitten?" Jamison asks as he stalks towards me.

I back up against the desk and the edge hits my thighs hard. I can't feel it though. My heart is racing too fast and I'm freaking the fuck out inside. Jamison looks menacing.

"Do you not comprehend simple requests?"
I look at him confused. What the fuck is he talking about?

"Let me put it in more simple terms for you to understand. Stay. The fuck. Away. From my brother," he says, enunciating each word. I know he just implied I am stupid and my blood boils as he hovers above me, glaring.

I point my finger in his face. "Don't fucking talk to me like I'm an idiot, Jamison."

He snatches my hand and squeezes it. "Aren't you though? That's why you lied about your credentials. Not even your pathetic hacking skills could hide that, could they?"

I'm too stunned to speak. This is the first time he's voiced anything out loud. Everything up until now has just been an unspoken accusation.

"What is so captivating about you that my dearest brother cannot seem to stay away?" He places his hand against his chin and thumbs his bottom lip like he's deep in thought. A smirk forms on his lip. "Maybe it is time for you to come clean," he continues.

My eyes go wide.

"Or does the rest of Bolt Corporation already know? Maybe you get on your knees for all of them, hmm."

"Fuck you," I seethe out, finally finding some semblance of words.

"I could be persuaded...to keep my mouth shut a bit longer."

My jaw drops. Is he fucking serious right now? Does he think I just blow everyone? I fucking earned my place here. I've done everything that has been asked of me and more.

"You have no issue fulfilling my brother's needs. What exactly is your issue now, Kitten? What do you do to him? You have him wrapped around your little finger. Do you think you guys are going to run away together one day? Maybe get married? Have a family? I'm his family." His last words come out a bit unhinged.

There it is. I see it now. The slight flash of jealousy in Jamison's eyes. Is he jealous that I'm taking his brother from him? Would he really say something now after all these years? It doesn't matter. I can't take that chance.

"Okay," I say.

"Okay?" He repeats like it's a question. He didn't think I would go through with this.

I drop to my knees in front of him. "Let me persuade you," I say before reaching for his buckle. He doesn't move a muscle, but I see the heat blaze in his eyes. I can tell he wants me. For revenge or pleasure, I'm not even sure. As I look up at him, I feel myself getting wet. He pushes a lock of hair out of my face gently. It's so unlike him I'm almost confused for a second.

"Such a good little slut, aren't you? On your knees just for me."

'*This is so wrong*,' I think as I nod up at him and unbuckle his pants. Why am I enjoying this? His zipper comes down and I reach in releasing his very large and very thick cock. The light from the window glints off the metal piercing crossed through the tip. *'Oh fuck,'* I think as I grip him and feel the set of piercings lining down the bottom of his entire shaft. To top it off, his dick is completely covered in an intricate tattoo design. I lean forward and lick the tip, tasting the drop of precum before wrapping my lips around his head and sucking. He groans and I swear the sound makes me whimper. Suddenly, he grips me by the hair and pulls me back off his cock.

"Tell me you are only on your knees for us."

I look at him confused.

"Tell me, Kitten. Say you're our little slut. Just for Jonathan and I."

Fuck, why does that sound so hot? I shouldn't be doing this. I certainly shouldn't be enjoying this. I nod yes.

"Say it. Use your words."

"Ye...yes. I'm only yours. Yours and Jonathan's."

He looks at me with such adoration I swear my knees would be weak if I wasn't already on them.

"Good girl. Now prove it," he says as he guides my mouth back onto his dick. And I want to. I want to prove it so bad right now. I slide my mouth all the way down, hollowing my cheeks and let it hit the back of my throat before pulling back and using my hand to twist around his shaft.

"Fuck, fuck," he groans as he pushes my head up and down, guiding my movements.

Jamison, unhinged and raw like this is incredible. I'm so wet, I'm practically dripping. I squirm as he uses my mouth like I'm his favorite toy.

"Touch yourself, Kitten. I want you to come on your fingers while I come down this pretty little throat."

I don't need to be told twice. I'm so worked up, I'm sure it won't take long before I burst. I keep a firm grip on his cock with one hand while I slide two of my fingers down between my legs and rub my clit. I can't help the moan that escapes my mouth.

"You like that? You like me fucking your little slut mouth while you touch your wet pussy?" Jamison groans out, while he proceeds to fuck my face. He grabs the bottom of my throat and my hair, completely taking control while he thrust in and out furiously. I ride my two fingers while rubbing my clit with my other hand all while he plunges in and out. Tears track down my face but I don't even care in this moment. I can feel the coil in my belly beginning to unravel as his thrusts become erratic.

"You're such a good little slut. Be a good girl and come with me," he grits out.

I'm not sure if it's his degradation, praise or the combination of both, but whatever it is, it sends me over the edge. I come with a cry around his cock, barely able to keep myself upright. He plunges one last time as I moan, shooting his cum straight down my throat. I swallow as he pulls out and tucks himself back into his pants. He squats down in front of me as I sit back on my heels, completely out of sorts. The look on his face is hard to decipher.

"You did well, Kitten." he says as he wipes his thumb across my bottom lip and proceeds to stand up.

I guess we are back to formal speaking. This man is an enigma.

"Jamison?" I ask as he grabs the handle of the door to leave.

He turns towards me but doesn't say anything.

"How much longer? How much longer will you keep my secret?" I ask him.

He turns back towards the door before answering me. "A bit longer, Kitten. I'm not sure I'm done with you yet." He leaves, the door shutting behind him, while I'm left on the floor wondering what the hell I have just gotten myself into.

Chapter 12

Jamison

My keys click annoyingly as I type on my computer. Backspace again for the third time. Fuck, I cannot get the image of Kaz on her knees for me out of my head. The feel of her lips wrapped around my cock so perfectly. That was not supposed to happen. My intentions were to get her to back off of Jonathan. I couldn't turn down the opportunity when it arose, though. She has some sort of hold of my twin. It is unhealthy. It is dangerous. The image of her taking me to the back of her throat flashes in my head again. I slam my palm down on my desk before grabbing the bottle of water I have and chugging it. She's a fucking sorceress. I can feel a migraine setting in. It has been at least fourteen hours since I last ate. The time on my clock reads six am. I push away from my desk and make my way to the kitchen before stopping in my tracks. Jonathan hums happily while messing with the coffee pot. He turns around and smiles big before leaning both hands against the counter behind him.

"Well good morning, brother. How nice of you to grace me with your presence today."

I ignore him and push my way into the kitchen before pulling eggs out of the fridge and heading towards the stove. I'm about to crack my third egg when he starts chuckling behind me. I whirl around with an egg in hand and see him smiling at his phone while sitting at the kitchen island. The egg cracks in my hand. Jonathan looks up at me, confused.

"Who are you texting that has you in such a happy state?" I grit out.

His eyes narrow. "None of your business. Also, you have

egg all over your hand."

I look down at my hand and notice I do indeed have egg running down my forearm. Stepping forward, I wash my hands and arm while still eyeballing my brother.

"That better not be Kaz."

Jonathan jumps up and places both hands on the counter leaning towards me. "So fucking what if it is. I'm sick of you telling me what to do. It's none of your business."

"Everything you do is my business," I growl.

"No. It. Isn't." He slams his palm down for effect. "We have had a thing for each other for years now. It hasn't affected the company. I know you know it. I'm sick of sneaking around. I want her, Jamison. She wants me too. I think we could have something special."

I smirk at him. "You think you are going to have something special with her? Do you think you're the only guy she has been sneaking around with, brother?"

Jonathan just stares at me as I pull my phone from my back pocket. I scroll my phone for the video I'm looking for before placing it across the counter in front of my brother.

"What the fuck is this?" he asks me as he gestures to my phone.

"Press play," I reply coolly.

He does as I say. The video shows the back of Kaz's hair wrapped around my fist. My phone is perfectly positioned on the desk behind her. You can't see her face but you can hear her moaning around my cock while I fuck her pretty little mouth. It's only a small portion of the full clip. Just enough to hear her come all over her own fingers while I shoot my cum down her throat.

Jonathan stands there staring at my phone, his jaw set.

"She is not special, brother. She is just like every other whore we decide to fuck around with. We only have each other."

He doesn't look at me but I know he's hurt and angry. A small price to pay to ensure he isn't blinded by pussy. He will get over it. He grabs his phone and throws it. It hits the wall and shatters into pieces. Without so much as a glance back in my direction, he stalks to his room and slams the door shut behind him. I grab my phone and exit the video before sending out a text message. A new phone will be delivered for Jonathan before the end of the day. I turn back to my now burnt eggs and clean the pan out while whistling to myself. I grab a banana and head back into my room while eating it. Victory never tasted so sweet.

Chapter 13

Jonathan

It's been over a month at least since I've responded to any of Kaz's messages. Normally I'm the one continuously messaging her but I really just can't right now. If i'm being honest with myself, I'm fucking hurt. I know we weren't ever an actual item. We have been towing this line between coworkers and I don't know… "lovers" for so long, I think I'm just so mixed up. There was never an official conversation, mostly because we were hiding from everyone, but also because Kaz only messaged me when she was tipsy. Everytime I think of it like that, it pisses me off. Had she been fucking with me all along? I mean, I never asked her to be exclusive but she could have at least had the decency to not mess around with anyone else at work. She made me think we had something special. Somewhere in the back of my mind I thought one day it would be more. Now, instead, I'm left wondering who else she's been fucking. Does she take turns blowing Sebastian with Sasha? What about Xavier? Maybe he fucks her on the side too. Andre? My brother? Both at the same time? The last part really gets me. I can feel my knuckles tighten, harshly gripping the pen I've been aimlessly flipping around. I've been stuck in my office all fucking day trying to avoid seeing her. Now I find myself flipping the shades so I can peer out hoping to catch a glimpse. She's nowhere around but the door to my office opens abruptly to my left and Xavier strides in.

"We are going to the new sex club that asshole Lockhart is opening this weekend. I'm getting a VIP setup so we can get a layout of the place and try to figure out what kind of pie he has his hands in."

"Is this mandatory?" I ask him while still staring through the glass. Kaz steps off the elevator onto our floor. She looks fantastic as usual in her tight skirt and ruffled blouse. She's got on a pair of sexy red heels and red lipstick to match. Visions of me fucking her while she wears those heels assault my memory. I squeeze my eyes shut in an attempt to clear my head.

"Jonathan, are you okay?" Xavier asks me.

I turn towards him with a curt smile that feels painted on and respond, "Yeah, I'm good man. Just have a headache." My head swivels right back to the glass eyeing Kaz as she steps up to Sebastian and starts showing him some paperwork.

"So will you be able to go? We could really use you and Jamison. More eyes to see what's going on." Xavier says casually while also looking through the glass. No doubt, he is looking directly where I am now. Sebastian places his hand on Kaz's lower back and guides her into his office before shutting the door behind him. I grind my molars and blow out a breath to try to control the slight rage I'm currently feeling.

"Count me in," I respond to Xavier finally.

He looks at me with a straight face for a good thirty seconds before I raise my brows at him in question.

"Sebastian isn't into Kaz. You know that right?"

I roll my eyes in irritation. "It's not my business who Sebastian is into. Besides, she's off limits, remember?"

He laughs at me and opens the door to my office. "Oh, I remember alright. I'm just not sure you ever actually heard the memo."

The door slams behind him leaving me to question if Kaz and I were ever as careful as I thought we were.

Chapter 14

Jamison

We've been sitting at Lock & Key in the VIP section for the past hour. Jonathan has made it his life's mission to get impossibly drunk tonight. He doesn't seem himself. Really, he hasn't seemed himself for the past month. I know it has to do with Kaz. He is still upset. I thought he would be over it by now, but it is like she has some invisible hold on my twin that I cannot seem to break. I cannot get her out of my head either. Over the past month I have found myself paying closer and closer attention to the things she is doing or saying. I can tell while my brother is avoiding her, she is also avoiding me. She cannot avoid me forever, though.

I'm feeling a little guilty tonight, Kitten. I may need a reminder of why I'm keeping your secret.

I watch as the three dots appear and disappear a few times before a message finally comes through.

You have no feelings, Jamison.

I smirk at her text. Kitten has her claws out tonight.

Now, now. That isn't true at all. For instance, I'm feeling quite a bit of something when I remember how perfectly your lips wrapped around my cock...

A few moments go by again before she responds.

I can't do this, Jamison. What if people find out?

I glare down at my phone. She means, what if Jonathan finds out. Jealousy hits me quickly. She does not have the slightest clue I showed him that video. Why hasn't he told her? I look up at my brother to see him pull a busty waitress down on his lap. Quickly, I snap a picture and send it to Kaz.

If you are worried about my brother, he is perfectly content.

Her response is immediate.

Fuck you both.

I hear my brother whisper in the waitress's ear asking her if she likes sandwiches. She giggles and leans into him. Suddenly, I'm filled with the visual of my brother and I while we both take Kaz. I wait for the jealousy to flare up, but it doesn't. In my mind, we are all there together and something about that doesn't sound so terrible after all. My phone flies out of my hand and hits the ground a few feet away. I look up to see my brother staring at me intently. This motherfucker just slapped my phone out of my hand. I hear a giggle and look down to see the waitress in my lap undoing my belt. Jonathan raises his brow at me.

"I'm going to need you to pay a little bit of attention to our blonde friend tonight, brother. Let her loosen up some of that tension you have going on." His words slur slightly as he speaks. I know exactly what he is doing right now. He is drowning himself the best way he knows how. Xavier and Sebastian both stare at me, waiting for a response. I am thoroughly pissed off at my brother, but now is not the time to have this discussion.

"Fine," I grit out and grasp the blonde's hair tightly in one hand while unzipping my pants with the other. She gasps in pain out loud, causing my dick to twitch. "Show me what's caught my brother's interest."

I close my eyes and envision Kaz, as the waitress reaches

into my pants. My dick thickens at record speed as she wraps her lips around it and sucks. I hear Sebastian and Xavier get up to leave and Jonathan calling out about taking our sweet time with this one but I pay little attention. I'm stuck in my head with my memories. My dick is so hard it could burst right now. I plunge into her wet mouth, causing her to gag. She gasps as Jonathan enters her from behind.

"Yes," she moans in a horrible high pitched voice making me cringe.

"Less talking," I say before grabbing her head and shoving her back onto my dick. "This isn't the time for a speech."

She looks up at me with wide eyes while Jonathan laughs from behind her. I need to make this quick before my dick decides to deflate. I look over at my brother who now has his eyes closed while he fucks this woman from behind. A look of ecstasy is on his face. Is he thinking of Kaz? Is he playing out a scene with the three of us instead of this blonde bimbo? I groan and close my eyes while playing those same thoughts out in my own head. It doesn't take long before my release is shooting down the waitress's throat. She sputters as I rip her mouth from my dick. A feeling of disgust has already settled into the pit of my stomach. Maybe I should have actually had a few drinks tonight. I stand swiftly, pushing myself around her and my brother.

"I have to use the restroom. I do not need anymore tension loosened, Jonathan."

Jonathan laughs in acknowledgement as I exit VIP. I make my way to the restrooms and spend the next ten minutes perusing the bottom floor before heading back up again. When I return, Jonathan is standing near the balcony, peering out over the edge with his phone in hand. I walk up next to him just as his phone buzzes.

"Who are you texting?" I ask him nonchalantly.

He looks at me, guilt crossing his features.

"Are you fucking serious? I thought we discussed this. You were just balls deep in that waitress. What could you possibly need from that little slut?"

"Don't call her that," he growls out. "I wasn't the only one balls deep. I thought I could get over her but not even fucking that waitress with you could get her out of my head. I think it made it worse!"

I don't miss the way he says "with you," insinuating that he thought us resuming our normal extracurriculars would fix this situation. I also cannot tell him he's wrong either. It did make it worse. If I thought she had a hold of us before, I was sadly mistaken. The thought of her between the both of us is searing itself into my brain. The only thing better than my imagination right now would be the real thing. Unfortunately, I may have already fucked that up and I'm not sure If It can be fixed now. I sigh and turn towards the crowd on the ground level.

"We should discuss this later when you have sobered up."

"Yeah, whatever," Jonathan says as he pockets his phone.

We both peer out into the crowd before my brother nudges me and points someone out by one of the bars. "Is that who I think it is?"

I look over to see Riley, Sebastian's intern, standing next to her husband. They look like they might be having a disagreement of sorts.

"I wonder if Sebastian knows she is here?" Jonathan asks curiously.

"Doubtful," I reply. "If he did, you know he would already be hovering somewhere close and I don't see him anywhere."

"True," Jonathan laughs.

We watch as Nate grabs a couple drinks from the bar and guides Riley into one of the private rooms on the side. Turning from the balcony, I stroll over and grab my phone from the floor and turn the screen on to see there still isn't a response from Kaz. Irritation flows through me but I push it away completely before making my way back over to Jonathan who looks ready to pass out against the wall.

"Come on, brother," I say, squeezing his shoulder. "I think it's time to call it a night."

Chapter 15

Kaz
One month later

I'm in the back of the Uber heading to the office, scrolling through my phone when a text from Riley comes through.

How are things in the office? I need to figure out how to get past all this. I'm going stir crazy.

I smile before shooting off my response.

I'm sure Sebastian is keeping you plenty busy. (Winking emoji)

Last month Riley was kidnapped by her psycho husband, Nate. They aren't divorced yet but she has definitely left him. I never liked the guy anyway. He is a total loser and didn't deserve someone as nice and as caring as Riley. She's been staying with my boss Sebastian who is completely head over heels for her. It's so funny to think of that man caring about anyone other than himself. I never thought I would see the day. The men of Bolt Corporation have never been the type to settle down but it seems that trend might be starting to take a turn. I think of Jonathan and the multiple texts I receive from him daily. I was starting to think he really did care until Jamison sent me that video last month with some skeezy bimbo on his lap. I was so pissed off I didn't speak to him for days. The funny part is, he didn't even bother lying to me about it once I finally decided to speak to him again. He fully admitted to fucking her…with Jamison. That was what really sent me over the edge. Jamison sent me that picture to fuck with my head. I hate him. I hate how calculated he is. I hate how god damn good looking he is even when his deep blue eyes scream psychopath. But most of all...I hate how turned on I was at the thought of me being between him and Jonathan instead of that girl. What is wrong with me? Maybe I am the slut he wants me to be. My phone vibrates pulling me from my thoughts and I look down to see it's Riley again.

You have no idea! But really, let's get together for lunch soon okay? And have the guys send me something to do before I go insane!

I respond back letting her know I will do my best to get her some work and of course we can figure out lunch just as my ride puls up out front of the office building. I wave bye to my driver and turn to walk up when I'm greeted by the most delicious sight of Jonathan getting off his sleek black motorcycle. He whips his helmet off causing his waves to fall forward. That messy hair combined with his unbuttoned suit and lack of tie give him the perfect 'I don't give a fuck' bad boy vibe. Why does he make looking good so damn easy? He turns towards me with his dazzling smile and bright blue eyes and I immediately school my features. I can't let him see me drooling dammit.

"Hey, Pretty Girl," he whispers as he walks up next to me casually and we both enter the doors to the building.

"Morning, Jonathan," I state in the most normal voice I can muster even though my insides are squirming at hearing him call me Pretty Girl.

He groans next to me and I look at him quickly before looking around. He's staring at me like I'm dessert. My cheeks go red.

"Fuck, you look so sexy in that outfit. What I wouldn't give to see what's under it."

I smirk at him as we enter the elevator and the doors begin to close.

"Nothing," I whisper.

His eyes go wide. "Fuck, Kaz I'm going to be hard all day now knowing you're commando. Please say you will meet me...."

His words are cut off by a hand halting the doors to the elevator. We both stare as Jamison steps on facing us both.

"Brother," he says, greeting Jonathan before turning towards me with a smirk. "Kaz."

I turn my head completely straight forward and don't acknowledge he is there. That pisses him off. I can practically feel the steam filling the elevator as the doors close and we descend. Shit, no one pressed the button and now we are heading to the basement.

I don't have time to think about stopping the elevator before Jamison growls out, "You can acknowledge my brother but not me? You did not seem to mind looking at me when my cock was down your throat though, did you, Kitten?"

My face goes beat red and I whip my eyes toward him, prepared to lay into him but Jonathan is faster. Suddenly, he has Jamison pushed up against the elevator wall, his hands gripping the collar of his perfectly pressed suit.

"Don't fucking talk to her like that," he grits out.

Jamison's eyes narrow on him before replying back. "I think she likes it when I speak to her that way. Her panties are probably drenched. She's just waiting for me to remind her of what a little slut she is."

And fuck if he's not right. I'm wet alright, but there isn't any underwear to catch the moisture collecting between my thighs. I'm vaguely aware of the elevator halting before ascending back up as I step up close and attempt to push them apart.

"You guys need to both calm down. We can't do this here at work."

They both look at me before each other and then Jonathan smirks and I already know his brother won't like his next words.

"Oh I know exactly how wet she gets, brother. I had her coming all over my face just last week."

The elevator goes silent and I close my eyes praying a black hole will come and swallow me up. Did I hook up with Jonathan last week after having far too many drinks when out with a few friends? I sure did. Am I still mad at him for screwing that bimbo? Yes, and no. We have never discussed being exclusive and had it been brought up, I would have said no anyway. I can't risk my job but most of all, I can't risk him finding out what kind of life I really come from. He wouldn't think twice about me if he knew my background. Suddenly the elevator door dings and we all turn towards it as it opens, revealing none other than Sebastian Bolt. He stands there staring at the three of us with his eyes narrowed. I remove my hands from both twins' chests before backing away guiltily. Jonathan and Jamison both step away from each other and face Sebastian.

"Everything okay here?" Sebastian asks, looking directly at me. I nod at him, unable to form a sentence. I'm scared shitless right now.

"Fine," I hear Jonathan mutter while I stare at the ground.

"Better than how it looks out there," Jamison says to Sebastian. I can hear the amusement in his voice and can only imagine he is giving him shit right now about his flustered appearance.

"Fuck off," Sebastian replies.

I close my eyes hoping to get to my floor as quickly as possible so I can get out of the awkward situation but Jamison is clearly on a mission which is completely unlike his normal stoic demeanor.

"Long night, boss?" he asks Sebastian, that hint of amusement still on the edge of his words.

My phone rings loudly cutting them off and I answer quickly seeing that it's Riley. Fuck yes, saved at last.

"Riley!" I say far too enthusiastically. "What are your plans today? Hang on, let me get to my desk." Never mind that we were just texting each other not more than fifteen minutes ago. The guys don't need to know those minor details. I step off the elevator and walk away quickly while she laughs on the other end of the line. I make my way to my office before setting up lunch plans with her for a few hours later.

It's about noon when I walk into the cozy little bodega to meet Riley and stop dead in my tracks. Riley and Sasha, Sebastian's most recent assistant, are both standing there looking to be in a very serious conversation. They must have been loud because other guests are starting to look in their direction. I usher them both over to some seats.

"Sasha," I say. "So lovely to see you again. I've been trying to track you down."

"Listen," Sasha starts, "I can't help you guys with my uncle. I can't tell you anything. It's dangerous just talking to you." She looks at Riley and I swear she does look remorseful. "About Nate...he'd made it seem like you guys were splitting up, Riley. And I just thought it would be fun."

Oof, I think to myself. Wrong thing to say, Sasha.

Riley glares at her. "Fun. Fucking someone's husband?"

"I made a mistake. But listen," Sasha's voice lowers and she continues, "I'm scared."

This makes me laugh out loud, causing both Riley and Sasha to look at me. This bitch is certifiable if she thinks we are going to believe anything she says. "You're scared?! Riley was fucking kidnapped and raped. By Nate!"

Riley sinks into her chair, looking defeated. My heart hurts for her. "Sasha, is Nate hurting you?" she asks.

"You need to leave, Riley. You need to leave the city," Sasha says, looking around like she's afraid we are being watched. Riley jumps up suddenly, causing me to jolt backwards.

"Fuck this," she says and storms towards the restroom.

I turn to Sasha and glare. "You have some fucking nerve."

"You don't understand, Kaz. You never will. You have people that care about you."

"You could have that too, Sasha, if you weren't such a conniving bitch," I grit out.

She stands up and places both hands on the table, glaring at me.

"You may have escaped your old life, but it won't ever work out so well for me."

My eyes widen and she looks at me determined. "That's right, my uncle knows about you, Little Devil. You better hope he doesn't start taking a liking to you or you and I will be in the same boat." Her eyes soften a little bit before she continues. "You and I might never have been best friends, but I wouldn't wish this life on anyone. Please, be careful." Before I can get the chance to respond, she has already made her way out the door. Not five minutes later, Riley runs up to me and grabs me by the arm, pulling me outside.

"Let's go, Kaz. Now!" she yells.

"Riley? What the hell? I just ordered lunch! I thought Sasha was having a nervous breakdown, then she just up and disappeared. I was about to give her a piece of my mind..."

I'm so flustered by what just happened that the lies just spew from my mouth like a volcano. Luckily, Riley seems just as flustered and doesn't question me as we make it about a block down the street and she hails a cab. We both get in and she turns to me.

"Kaz, Nate was in the bathroom. He's after me. We need to call Sebastian."

I feel like I'm in a movie right now and it takes a good minute to register what has just happened.

"Oh my god, Riley! Are you okay?? Did he touch you?"

"I'm okay," she replies."But I don't have my phone. Can you call him for me?"

The cab driver glances in the rearview mirror at her but says nothing as I dial Sebastian.

"Where the fuck is Riley?" Sebastian's voice cuts through the phone.

"I'm okay, Sebastian, thanks for asking. Here's Riley," I reply sarcastically before handing the phone over. I completely zone out while they speak, mulling over Sasha's words. She called me Little Devil. I haven't heard that name since I left home. Since I stopped fighting. My best friend's face flashes in my head and I close my eyes to keep from having a complete meltdown. They never found him. They never found a body and I've just been here living my life pretending my past doesn't exist. My fingers trail the length of my skirt and pass over a spot on my thigh. The familiar itch for the cold metal against my skin hits me. I've become too complacent. I've gotten too used to this lifestyle, thinking I was safe. I'm not safe. Lockhart knows who I am, and if he knows, that means other people know.

We make it to the apartment, both of us quiet, as we head up. I think we both must be in shock as we sit on the couch and wait. I'm unsure how much time passes before the door swings open and the guys all rush in. Both Jamison and Jonathan head over to me looking worried. Jamison looks worried? I'm so confused by that while Jonathan offers to check me for injuries. I laugh internally, even though I can't seem to muster up an emotion on the outside. This man has no idea how well I can actually take care of myself. Had I seen Nate at the restaurant, he certainly wouldn't have been leaving so easily. The guys must both notice how out of it I am as they lead me out the door and offer to take me home.

They walk me up, even though I tell them no, and I can see by the look on both of their faces, they are questioning if I'm really okay. Am I? I'm not really sure but I can't look at either of them right now. I can't look at both of them while they treat me like I'm some delicate flower when I know damn well I'm not. When I know I've been hiding this part of me for so damn long, I'm sure it's about to burst free. So I close the door on both of their faces and I pull the little shoebox out that's been stuffed in the back of my closet for years. My fingers run over the thin bands of the thigh strap before gliding over the edge of the small dagger. I smile as I look her over, noting the etching in the side. *'Little Devil'* it reads.

I sure missed you baby.

Chapter 16

Jamison

Two months later

"Where is Sebastian?" Andre's voice comes over the video chat in our meeting room.

Xavier laughs beside me before replying. "He took the day off."

I catch a glimpse of Andre rolling his eyes. "Must be nice to go gallivanting around town with your fiance' when there's business to attend to."

"Don't you have like ten fiancés, bro?" My twin, Jonathan jokes beside me.

Andre breathes out a sigh from over the line and ignores him before continuing on about a few new hires and paperwork needing to be looked over. Jonathan jumps in a little too eagerly.

"I can go over all of that with Kaz."

"Not so fast," Xavier says. "We have that case you were supposed to be helping me with. I need to go over a few more documents with you. This one is important and it aligns with one of Sebastian's other cases." He pauses for a minute before turning to me. "Any chance you can look over it with Kaz?"

Jonathan looks thoroughly annoyed which gives me a small sense of satisfaction. He spends far too much time with her anyway. It's quite obvious he is purposely separating his time between us and I don't like it. I lick my lips and look around like I'm pondering in my head while Xavier watches me from the side. A small smirk tilts just the edge of my mouth as I stare directly into my twin's eyes. His bright blue eyes shine even brighter in anger, but he says nothing. He already knows I am going to accept. He always knows, even when he doesn't want to.

"I'm sure I can spare a bit of time in my schedule today," I respond.

Xavier and Andre both blow out breaths of relief. I can see Andre stand up at his desk on his screen. "Well, if I'm not needed for anything else, I'm going to sign off. Let me know when our CEO decides to grace us with his presence.

"Will do," Xavier laughs, also standing up. He looks at Jonathan, clearly sensing something amiss in the air. "You okay, man?"

"I'm fricking fantastic," he replies sarcastically before getting up and walking out.

"Umm, okay then. Guess I'll get with him later. I'm out."

I nod my head without replying out loud. I'm already focused on the message I'm sending to Kaz.

I'm coming down to your office to go over that paperwork.

Her reply comes in quickly.

What? No. Xavier is going to.

My eyes narrow at her text. Who does she think she is? It is quite clear I've become a bit too lax with her recently.

Xavier is busy.

This time her response takes a few minutes longer. Almost like she's nervous and unsure what to do with my short reply. Good. She should be nervous.

I'll come to your office. Heading up now.

'Even better,' I think as I stroll to my office and settle in my chair. Not more than five minutes pass before Kaz storms into my office, slamming the door shut behind her. She huffs out as she slams a few files down on my desk and puts one hand on her hip, glaring at me. My face remains neutral as I peruse her body. She's wearing plain black close-toed heels and a black pin skirt that rests just above her knee. There's a slit on one side that barely rises a few inches up. Her blouse is a deep blue color that cuts down just enough to show a hint of cleavage. It's so fucking classy and sexy all at once, it's a wonder my dick doesn't rip a hole in my pants right here. I see her swallow nervously as I stare at her.

"Clearly, you are getting far too comfortable with me and are beginning to forget a few key points."

She narrows her eyes at me before speaking. "What the fuck are you talking about, Jamison?"

I lean back in my chair and cross my arms, raising my brows. She stops herself from speaking again, thinking better of whatever she was going to say.

"I think you need a reminder," I say as I rub my jaw with one hand. "On your knees."

"You can't be fucking serious," she seethes out. "No. This is ridiculous. You can't force me to suck you off every single time I piss you off. I should report you."

I look at her impassively. "That's fine. Would you like me to call our CEO now for you? You could let him know you're reporting me for sexual harassment. You could also let him know about your resume? Maybe tell him there are a few things on there that aren't supposed to be? I'll be sure to send him a video or two as well. Maybe one with you already on your knees for me, moaning like a slut while you ride your own fingers. I'm sure he will need it for evidence when you open your case against me…right?"

Her eyes are wide while I speak. Once I finish she leans over and grips the edge of my desk, giving me the most delectable view down her shirt. "There's something wrong with you."

"Tell me something I don't already know, Kitten," I reply as I brace both hands on the armrests of my chair and look down. She doesn't move.

"On. Your. Knees. Make your choice."

"As if I even have one," she huffs out before walking around my desk and dropping to the floor.

I lean over, gripping her around her neck, and get in her face. "Don't act like you don't enjoy this. Your pussy is probably gushing already at the thought of me choking you with my cock." Her eyes remain narrow and she doesn't respond so I pull my chair forward a bit more forcing her to sit further under my desk.

"What are you doing?" She asks, trying to push the chair back further.

"Clearly this is going to take a while and I have some files to go over, don't I?" I say as I grab one of the files and open it, shielding her from my view. My zipper is suddenly yanked down hard and I feel her aggressively pull my dick from my pants. Fuck, she doesn't even know what she's doing to me right now. She doesn't waste time with pleasantries. There's no warming me up with small licks or kisses. No, she is on a mission as she wraps her lips completely over my dick and sucks her mouth down on it as far as it can go.

"Fuck," I grit out as my upper body strains back against the chair and my palm slams down on my desk. She doesn't relent as she twists both of her palms around my base and continues to pump her mouth up and down. I grit my teeth and slam the file down, grabbing her by the back of her hair and wrenching her mouth off of me.

"Easy, Kitten. I'm trying to commit this to memory right now and I can't do that if I blow my load down your pretty throat in the first minute like a virgin schoolboy."

She looks at me devilishly, like that was her plan all along. Bad Kitten.

"Show me you know how to listen like a good girl," I say as I guide my dick back into her mouth. She sucks the head and swirls her tongue around making me groan out. "Fuck, thats good."

"Hey, Jamison, I need you to look at this real quick,"

Xavier says as he strolls into my office.

Kaz shrinks back further under the desk at the same time I push my chair completely forward. She attempts to pull her mouth from me but I grab the back of her neck and grip her tightly to keep her in place. Both of her palms come down on my thighs, roughly squeezing.

"Sure Xavier, what can I help you with?"

He hands me a paper that I hold with one hand while I continue to use my other hand to guide Kaz's head leisurely up and down my dick. I'm fucking savoring the way her warm, wet mouth encases me so perfectly. I also know there's no way in hell she is coming out from under this desk right now and taking the chance of getting caught. Xavier is completely unaware of the situation as he hovers over the front of my desk, pointing out a few things while he explains. From out of nowhere, Kaz's mouth tightens on my dick and she sucks me in deep. I attempt to pull her head back but she has apparently decided she isn't going to listen like I thought she would. She pumps up and down furiously making me grip her hair hard. She's got both hands wrapped around me again as she twists and sucks me so far down, I can feel myself hit the back of her throat. I can't think straight while she's sucking me off like I'm the last popsicle on a hot, desert island. Suddenly, my thighs tense up and the familiar tingle of an orgasm rips down my spine with absolutely zero warning. Kaz holds my cock in the back of her throat and swallows at the same time. I brace my other hand on my desk and drop the paperwork before gritting out another "fuck."

Xavier stops talking and looks at me quizzically. "Everything okay?"

"Umm yeah," I let go of Kaz under the table and run both palms down my face. "I'm good."

"You sure man? You look a little pale."

"I'm..." My thought is interrupted by the feel of Kaz sucking my half hard dick back into her mouth again. I groan a little out loud, internally cringing at what it must sound like. It seems Xavier really does think I'm unwell.

"Maybe you should go home. We can discuss this tomorrow. I don't want to get sick ya know?" He grabs the paperwork from my desk and towards the door quickly opening it. "I'll umm lock the door so no one else comes in here. We can't have anyone else catch something from you either. We're too busy right now for an office plague." He locks the door exiting quickly. As soon as the door slams closed, I push my chair back quickly and unfasten my tie.

"You think that was funny, Kitten?" I ask when Kaz smirks.

"That's what you get for forcing your dick down my throat in the first place, Jamison," she replies as she pushes herself up from her knees to her feet. She attempts to smooth her skirt down but I'm too quick. Before she knows it, I have her pushed up against my desk, her skirt pulled up and over her hips. I grab her by the throat roughly.

"You were a very bad girl." My hand trails up her thigh before coming into contact with cool metal. My hand grips the handle of a small dagger before pulling it free from its sheath and holding it between us. Kaz's whole body stiffens and I smile wickedly. With one quick motion, I slice the band on her panties and they fall to her feet, one side still hanging on her ankle. Both of her hands grip my wrist but she doesn't make a play to remove my hand from her throat.

"I'm going to show you what happens when you don't listen," I whisper as I trail her dagger down her cheek, neck and then to her cleavage. She squeezes my wrist tighter and I feel her knees buckle a little. Interesting. In a flash, I have her spun around and bent completely over my desk with my hand in her hair and my whole body pressed against her. My dick is once again at full mast. She pushes her ass back against me involuntarily.

"That's right, Kitten. You can pretend you don't want this all you want," I say, as I run my dick up and down her soaking slit and press the head just barely inside her. She wriggles around and a small moan escapes her lips. I lean down further and bite the shell of her ear. "You can pretend, but we both know you're a slut for Jonathan and I." She freezes at my last words, but I don't give her a chance to react as I slam my dick inside her, sheathing myself fully. Fuck, I've waited so long for this.

"Oh fuck," she moans, as I pump in and out of her.

"Not too loud or someone will hear you," I chuckle and shove my tie inside her mouth. She bites down on it, moaning into the fabric.

"You're so fucking wet. Is this because Xavier was in here too? Did you like him being in here while you sucked my dick?"

She shakes her head no.

"Don't lie to me you little slut. You're practically gushing. Should I call him back in here? Maybe you want us both?"

She continues to shake her head no while I run my thumb down her ass crack and rub against her puckered hole. I press the tip in just a little and watch as it clenches around me while my dick slides in and out of her pussy.

"I bet you'd like it if Jonathan joined us though, wouldn't you?"

She freezes causing me to chuckle as I press my thumb further into her ass.

"I wonder if you could take us both? In your pretty little pussy and your tight little ass."

She moans, my tie muffling the sounds, as I pump my dick and thumb in and out of her in tandem. "Do you want to come, Kitten?"

She nods her head yes as she pushes her ass back, fucking herself on my dick and thumb.

"Only good girls get to come. Are you a good girl? Are you going to behave now?"

I pull her head back so I can see her face and watch as her eyes flutter open. They are glassy as fuck and she looks absolutley beautiful like this. Completely blissed out.

"Admit you'd like it if Jonathan and I both took you together."

She doesn't say anything.

"Admit it and I'll let you come," I growl out as I pull her head up further.

Tears stream down her face as she shakes her head and moans what I'm fairly certain is a yes into the fabric.

"Good girl," I say, letting go of her hair. She falls forward, gripping the top of the desk edge with both hands. I use one hand to rub her clit quickly while pumping my thumb and dick inside her. She throws her head back, moaning, and I feel her pussy clench tightly. It pulsates around my cock, sending me over the edge. I come so hard, I nearly black out and bite down on Kaz's shoulder to stifle the sound of my moan. She doesn't move as I pull out and step back enough to watch my cum as it slowly drips out of her pussy and down her thighs. I run my fingers down her slit in awe of how fucking perfect it looks but my view is cut off quickly when she spins around and pulls her skirt down.

"You didn't use a condom."

"You're on birth control," I state matter of factly.

"How the hell do you know?" she asks me, angrily.

I tuck myself back into my pants and sit down in my chair looking up at her. "I know everything you do, Kaz. Everything. Now go clean yourself up." I wave my hand, dismissing her.

"You are a fucking asshole," she seethes as she throws my wet tie in my face, grabs her dagger, and shoves it back into its sheath. She then proceeds to grab a tissue and wipe under her eyes and around her mouth before dropping it on my desk. She looks directly at me while straightening her skirt and making it a point to not wipe my cum from her thighs before whipping around and strolling right out of my office with her head held high. I groan and bite my fist as I imagine it dripping from her the rest of the day. A reminder of who she belongs to.

Chapter 17

Kaz

Two Months later

I'm walking into my apartment and throwing down my gym bag when my phone vibrates. I roll my eyes when I look at it to see it's Jamison. I swear, his timing is impeccable. It's as if he's following me or something. He can wait, I think to myself, before peeling off my clothes and stepping into the shower. My muscles ache in the best way possible after the intense training I had today. Three months ago, I found a small MMA gym not far from where I live. When I first attended, I tried to play it off like I was new but I couldn't fool Enrique. To be fair, It had been way too many years since I had trained and I really had no idea how quickly I would pick it back up. He had me back and better than ever within the first month. I think the combination of Nate attempting to kidnap Riley yet again coupled with Xavier and Corrine's car accident really set me into motion.

Everyone knows that the accident was no accident at all. In fact, I'm pretty sure it was Lockhart's way of trying to get back at Sebastian and Riley for getting married. Since then, I've been laying low and attempting to watch my back as best as possible. The old me, the one that grew up on the bad side of the tracks, has come out and I'm not sure if that's a good or a bad thing just yet. The hot water hits my body and I sigh out loud relishing in the feel of it hitting my sore muscles. Before long, I've steamed up the entire bathroom. It billows out from the doorway as I reenter my bedroom and pick up my phone. My towel is wrapped around me and my hair lays wet against my back. Multiple unread messages show on my screen including one from Riley.

We are having a shopping day tomorrow! My sister could use a little retail therapy and I just know you are perfect to help me keep her company!

    I smile before shooting off a text agreeing to go with them. I'm actually pretty excited. It's been a while since I've gotten to just hang out with the girls and I really could use some retail therapy myself. Unfortunately, my dreams are crushed upon reading the text messages from Jamison I had ignored earlier.

Good evening Kitten.

Looks like I will be accompanying you and the girls tomorrow.

You are clearly ignoring me. I'll add it to the list of punishable offenses.

    I bite my lip and rub my thighs together remembering the last time Jamison had punished me in his office just a few weeks earlier. He had forced me to my knees right under his desk and unzipped his pants. Before I knew what was happening, his dick was halfway down my throat while he whispered the dirtiest things to me. The worst part was Xavier walking in and Jamison deciding it was the perfect time to have a five minute conversation with him. I was so mortified at being caught under Jamison's desk, yet completely turned on at the same time, that I continued to suck him off. Once Xavier had left and locked the door behind him, he had immediately pulled me out from under his desk and bent me over the top. That was the first time I actually slept with Jamison. He was an entirely different animal. Shoving his tie in my mouth while fucking me ruthlessly. I remember him calling me a little slut and asking me if I wanted Xavier to come back and join us. I had shaken my head no angrily and glared at him. He had laughed and asked me if I preferred

Jonathan instead. I didn't respond to that particular question right away but he knew my truth. Once we were done, he had dismissed me without a second thought, telling me to go clean myself up. Fucking asshole. I was so pissed off I went home early that day and spent twice the time at my gym. I fucking hate him. I hate that he holds my secret over my head and I hate that my body responds to all of the dirty things he does to it. How can two humans who have shared the same womb be so different? Jonathan, so sweet and light hearted. Jamison, so dark and twisted. Another text comes through making me chuckle while rolling my eyes.

Bad Kitten.

I throw my phone down on my nightstand without responding back to him. If I have to have a babysitter, I might as well make it fun. And what's more fun than getting under Jamison's skin? If he wants to play games, I'll show him that two can play.

Chapter 18

Jamison

She's fucking with me, I know it. I watch Kaz as she struts past the assistant's desks, casually looking in my direction with a glint in her eye. She's wearing a pair of strappy heels and a short pin skirt with her signature ruffled blouse. I don't give her the satisfaction of knowing she's getting to me as I watch her while leaning against the doorway of my office. Internally, my brain is on overdrive. I keep imagining her in the sexy little piece of lingerie she tried on last week when she was shopping with the girls. Visions of her dancing with Corrine, Riley's sister, at the club assault my memory and I scowl. She was trying to piss me off and she succeeded. I can't wait to punish her again. I thought I was enamored by her before, but now that I've really had a taste, I don't think I can let her go. The problem is that neither can Jonathan. We have shared every damn thing our entire lives yet this woman is destroying that piece by fucking piece. I watch as she enters Xavier's office and my eyes narrow. She better not be letting Xavier fuck her too. A few minutes go by and she doesn't exit. She wouldn't dare, would she? So many secrets, my Kitten has. Could this be another? I stride towards the office casually but pick up my pace when I hear Xavier shouting at Kaz. I stop for a minute and listen to their conversation before entering.

"Why don't you head back up to your office and I'll bring the proper documents by in a bit, Kaz?" I say to her curtly.

I grab her arm to stop her as she proceeds to glide past me. "Are you okay?"

"Don't act like you care now," she says with a dirty look

before pulling her arm away and walking out. She will pay for that comment later.

I walk into Xavier's office fully and shut the door behind me. Might as well take the opportunity to inform him of some other issues I've come across. I lean against the door and pull out my pocket knife to clean out underneath my nails.

"We have a problem," I state.

"No fucking shit," is his response. "What's the issue?"

"I finally got a ping on Sasha's phone."

He looks at me confused. "Why is that a problem? We have been looking for her this whole time, hoping to get some answers from her about Lockhart. Right? This means we can finally go find her and ask some much needed questions."

My face shows zero emotion but inside I'm yet again a raging inferno. My next words come out so crisp and blunt. No doubt, I will have to approach my brother a little more delicately.

"Her phone's location is pinging at The Cellar."

"Fuck," he says blowing out a breath.

"Fuck indeed," I respond.

"Do Andre or your brother know yet?"

I slip my knife back into my pocket and turn to open the door to leave. "No, I called a meeting today at two. I just happened to be near your office and heard the commotion. I figured I would tell you while I was here. I have a few things to do beforehand but I'll see you later… Oh, and Xavier? Don't ever yell at Kaz like that again." I don't give him a chance to respond before I leave and head back to my office, shutting myself in. I pull up a few feeds and spend the next hour reviewing the camera's I have placed strategically throughout Kaz's apartment, her office, her car and also the gym she's been going to recently. She thinks I don't know what she's been up to but she's sadly mistaken. I've been watching my Kitten like a hawk. I know everywhere she goes and everything she does. So many secrets, I wonder how she's been able to keep up this act all these years. Her resume with the prestigious school she graduated from. Fake. The hometown she grew up in. Fake. The wealthy family she has that no one ever sees and that she never visits even though she takes time off from work claiming vacation. Fake. I know for a fact she takes her vacation and spends the entire time holed up in a hotel room by herself. She's so afraid I'm going to spill one secret, she doesn't realize I already know them all. I've known them all and I won't tell a soul. Maybe at first I thought about it, I really did. I'll continue to hold it over her head because the sick part of me that craves her, loves her on her knees. The other part of me, the part I locked away a long time ago is afraid. Afraid she will realize I'm not going to tell and decide to leave anyways. I don't think my brother could handle it and I'm fairly certain I won't do any better.

Chapter 19

Jonathan

Sebastian fills another shot glass with whiskey and pushes it towards me. I eyeball it while having an internal battle inside of my head. That will be my fourth shot. I'm no lightweight but I know once I hit four, it's harder to stop.

"I know I'm not the normal man to air feelings out to, but are you okay?" Sebastian asks me with a perplexed look.

I laugh out loud while he maintains his look of confusion. "Do you forget who my twin is? Trust me Sebastian, if I were to air out my feelings, rest assured, that you at least wouldn't be last on my list."

He smirks while replying, "Well I guess you got me on that one."

I take the shot and quickly down it while he downs his. Both of our eyes trail to the sliding glass doors that head out to the balcony of my apartment. Kaz stands out there absentmindedly scrolling on her phone. Damn she looks good in her casual leggings and oversized t-shirt. I lick my lips, not realizing I'm doing it. The feel of eyes on me has me turning back to see Sebastian watching me.

"I'm okay man, promise."

His phone must vibrate in his pants because he pulls it out and smiles while typing. It must be Riley. I'll have to thank her later for getting me out of this potentially awkward conversation about my feelings. Maybe a fruit basket would suffice. Lord knows she deserves it with all of the bullshit she's had to endure. Not to mention how well she's managed to tame down Sebastian's asshole demeanor. That thought has my eyes traveling back to Kaz. Being with her all of these years, even in secrecy, has tamed me a bit too. Too bad we have to keep shit under wraps. I wish I could show her off to the world. I sigh before looking back to Sebastian as he continues to text.

"You don't have to stay here, ya know?"

He stops what he's doing and looks up at me.

I gulp. Hopefully he doesn't catch on to what I'm currently thinking. "You could go home. I mean it doesn't take two of us to watch Kaz. She can stay here for now and once we get word from everyone else, I can bring her home or whatever." I shrug my shoulders nonchalantly. Inside, I'm fucking praying he agrees.

"I guess you're right." He looks back at his phone before finishing. "Okay yeah. If you got this, I'll head back to the office. I'm sure it won't be more than a few hours before we hear anything anyway, and I have a few things I need to do."

'Fuck yes!' I think in my head while keeping a straight face.

"Cool man, okay I'll see you in a bit."
Sebastian nods and gets up. He waves towards the balcony at Kaz who is currently looking inside confused. He walks out my front door just as she's coming in.

"Where is he going?" she asks me.
I shrug my shoulders, acting like I didn't just conveniently cause this current situation, before sliding out of my seat and walking up to her.

"Have I told you tonight how fucking sexy you look?" I ask her as I cup her jaw and run my thumb across her bottom lip.

She huffs. "I'm still mad at you. But I guess you can shower me with a few compliments."

"It meant nothing," I reply guilty. "I swear it. I was drunk and hurt. You know I've only ever wanted you, Pretty Girl."

Her face softens as she gazes up at me. "I know, Jonathan. And I know I have no right to be mad when I did what I did with Jamison. I think we should talk about some things. I need to tell…."

I cut her off with my lips pressed against hers. Pulling away just a little. "You don't need to explain. I'm well aware of what my brother looks like." A twinge of jealousy flicks through me.

"That's not what I was..." I cut her off again. This time I plunge my tongue inside her mouth and pull her body flush against mine causing her to moan. There's a sudden vibration against my side and I look down to see Kaz's phone lit up in her hand she had attempted to grab me with.

Jamison's name shows up on her notification.

"What the fuck does he want?" I growl out before grabbing her phone and unlocking it. She doesn't make a play to grab it back as I read his message.

Are you being a good little Kitten for my brother or a dirty little slut?

I silently fume while Kaz stands there biting her lips. Her eyes are wide even though she hasn't read his message. I get the feeling she already knows what type of message she would be receiving from my brother. I type back a response.

She is perfectly fine. And don't call her a fucking slut.

Three dots appear and disappear before reappearing again. Not thirty seconds later I'm reading his next text message.

Well, hello brother. I just call it like I see it. Why don't you ask our little slut if she minds my little nickname for her? Better yet, how about you let her read my text and when she finishes do me a favor, yeah? Run your fingers through her pretty little folds and send me a picture of your glistening fingers.

I groan and look up at Kaz's worried face. Fuck, why did that sound so hot? I can feel my rock hard dick straining against my pants. I close my eyes in an attempt to calm myself down but I can't get the picture of Kaz on her knees for Jamison out of my head. I never cared about any of the girls we fucked before. I just wanted this one thing for myself and now he is doing his damndest to fuck it up for me. The bastard doesn't even care about her, I'm sure of it. I pause for a second while pondering that thought. Surely, he doesn't care about her? But if he did? I couldn't choose between them. He's my brother, my other fucking half, but her? I love her. I fucking love her and she doesn't even realize it yet. I'm not willing to give either of them up.

"Jonathan?" My name leaves her lips like a question and pulls me from my thoughts. I look at her in silence while she stands there nervously playing with the hem of her shirt.

"What...what did your brother say?" she asks me quietly. I realize she's moved further away from me while I've been thinking so I step closer to her causing her to back up again. The backs of her knees hit the edge of the couch and she has no choice but to sit and look up at me. Suddenly, I need to know. I need to know if he's right.

"He called you a little slut," I reply to her. Her eyes widen and I can see her throat muscles work as she swallows. "He called you our little slut, Kaz. So tell me, Pretty Girl, are you a little slut? Are you ours? Do you like it when my brother talks to you like that?"

Her face flushes and her lips part and I just know I have my answer before any words leave her mouth.

"Jonathan..." She attempts to speak but I silence her, pressing two fingers against her lips.

"I'm in agony here baby, so before you say whatever you are about to, I just need to know one thing..." My words trail off while I look her over. She looks so fucking sexy, all flushed and vulnerable right now. The thought of Jamison here with us whips through my mind as I drop to my knees in front of her and grab the edges of her leggings.

"If I remove your pants and wrap these beautiful legs of yours around my head. If I run my tongue up your pretty little pussy and find it soaking wet. Will it be for both of us, Pretty

Girl?" I look up at her with my brow raised. She pauses a moment before hesitantly nodding her head yes, and fuck if my dick doesn't instantly get harder. She still wants me but I need to hear it.

"Say it," I growl out as I yank her leggings off and she grabs the couch with both hands to keep from falling backwards. I grab her with both hands and run my thumb across her bare pussy, feeling her wetness coat it.

"It's for both of you," she whispers, looking away embarrassed. I grab her jaw forcing her to look down at me while I'm on my knees for her.

"Watch me," I say as I lift both legs over my shoulders and lean in. "Right now, my brother isn't here and I want you to watch me while I devour you. I want the satisfaction of knowing I'm the one who will bring you to ruin while you come all over my face."

She sucks in a breath just as I dive in. I feast on her like she's my last meal. I lick up her folds and flick my tongue against her clit before diving down and tongue fucking her. She moans and grabs my hair, holding me close while rocking against my face. I'm pleasuring her right now but I know it's not just me in her head, and for some reason, in this moment, I don't give a fuck if she's imagining Jamison here with us. Not one ounce of jealousy hits me as I pull my dick free from my pants and stroke it while she rides my face. She rolls her hips against me and her body shutters as she explodes, her thighs gripping my head in a vice. I'm so hard, I could fucking burst. She doesn't get a chance to catch her breath as I grab a condom from my wallet and lift her onto the back edge of the couch, impaling her with my dick in one swift motion.

"Jonathan, shit…" she moans out as I thrust into her quickly. She's so fucking wet, yet still it's a tight fit.

"Fuck, Pretty Girl. Your pussy is so tight and wet. It's taking my dick so well." I hold her to me as I pump in and out of her. I know I won't last much longer with how fucking worked up I am right now. "Show me what a good girl you are. Come for me again baby." I rub her clit as I feel the familiar tingle of an impending orgasm. Her thighs tighten and her walls clench tighter around my dick.

"Yes, fuck yes. Just like that," she moans and those words send me over the edge. My balls draw up and I come with a guttural moan right after she explodes from her own orgasm.

I nuzzle her neck, my softening dick still inside her. "You're so fucking perfect, Pretty Girl."

"Jonathan...we still need to talk," she sighs.

I laugh. "Listen, I was trying to talk, but then you had to go and attack me, and now here we are."

"I'm serious," she says, rolling her eyes.

"I know. Can we raincheck this?" I ask her, my eyes pleading as I pull out of her. I remove the condom and nip her lip playfully, before pulling my sweatpants back up, and disposing of it in the kitchen trash. I turn back to find her watching me curiously. "Look, I'm aware we need to have a more serious conversation. I have a lot on my mind, but right now, I could use a distraction from everything outside of this room. How about we table this conversation in favor of some pizza. Tomorrow we can get back to the real world?"

She smiles before grabbing her leggings and pulling them back on. "Okay, deal. One condition though...You better order mushroom because I'm starving and it's my favorite."

"Already on the way," I say, smiling as I walk back over and yank her to the couch. "How about a movie while we wait?"

"Sounds perfect, Jonathan."

Chapter 20

Jamison

We've just entered the casino portion of The Celler when Andre and Xavier walk away from us heading in the opposite direction from where we are walking.

"Where are they going?" I murmur quietly to Antonio as I watch them disappear through a set of double doors. He doesn't know it yet, but I already know exactly where they're heading. I have this place memorized like the back of my hand and have since the first time I was brought here at twelve years old. I grimace as the flashback assaults me.

"I'm hungry," Jonathan says to our parents as we sit in a small room with only one mirror on it. "When are we getting dinner?"

"There's no eating before a Cellar event, Jonathan. I already told you I would get whatever you guys want afterwards," our adopted father replies. He turns toward our adoptive mom and mutters under his breath, "Can't have them getting sick and puking everywhere." She rolls her eyes and walks out the only door as he holds it open for her. The door slams and I hear the distinct sound of a latch sliding. My eyes narrow as I assess the room around us. It has a large flat screen television set up with multiple game consoles. An entire rack of games and movies line one wall. There's a small sofa in front of the television. There is an entire area in the opposite corner full of various types of toys including Legos on top of a rug that expands the length of the room. My nose wrinkles. Why are we here? Our adoptive parents told us we were going somewhere fun. This place looks questionable even to my twelve-year old eyes. I

scan the wall with the mirror as Jonathan immediately heads to the television to flip it on. I've heard of these before when reading my mystery novels. If I had to guess, I'm betting it's a window and we are currently being watched.

"Come on Jamison. They have Call of Duty on here. Help me pass the time."

I groan as I turn to my brother and oblige his demand. I'm either bored or I'm bored. I can't really win in this situation. I'm unsure how much time has passed but the door swings open and two figures enter, both wearing hoods. The shorter figure pulls his hood down to reveal a set of hazel eyes and rather, large round nose. His pudgy features, combined with his twisted smile, immediately give me the ick. The figure beside him doesn't remove his hood, but stands there with his hands crossed in front of him. There's a tattoo on one of his hands of a woman's face wrapped in barbed wire. Interesting.

"I want that one." The pudgy man says to the other while pointing at my brother.

My hackles immediately rise. "What's going on?" I ask as I step in front of my brother.

"Don't worry, boy." The pudgy man laughs. "You're just as pretty, and I'm sure you will be called on soon. I would take you both, but I can't afford your steep prices."

I grimace at his last words, and bile rises in the back of my throat as I turn to my brother, who looks just as worried and confused as I am. The hooded figure makes a grab for my brother as the pudgy man exits the room and I slap his hand away.

"Don't touch him," I growl out, which pisses him off. He slams his palm against my chest with such force I'm thrown to the ground. I make to jump up quickly, but the last thing I see is Jonathan's wide eyes as he's carried out of the room like a sack of potatoes. I try the door but it's locked and in a fit of rage I find myself screaming at the top of my lungs, banging on the glass in front of me. I can't say how much more time passes, but I know my voice is hoarse and my knuckles are split, when the same hooded figure with the hand tattoo comes back in with a woman around my adopted mother's age. She smiles, her white teeth looking completely out of place next to her large nose. Her beady eyes, spaced far too wide for her face, scan my body, making me internally cringe. I scowl at her as she approaches me and pushes my normally groomed hair out of my face.

"Hello Jamison," she says as she pushes her over processed bleach blonde hair off of her shoulder and leans in close. "I'm Chanelle." Her eyes shoot to my bruised and bloodied knuckles, and she bites her lip before turning to the hooded figure. "He's perfect."

I'm ripped from my memories by Antonio nudging me to sit down at a poker table. He eyes me warily. "Where did you go just now?"

"Nowhere," I reply with zero emotion. I pull the chair out beside him and lean back while he places his bet, looking at me curiously. Our job was to scout the main area while Andre and Xavier make their way through the private rooms. I won't be sitting here, though. I have unfinished business to attend to, and nothing is going to get in my way.

"Where's the restroom?" I ask Antonio casually, while glancing around.

He nods his head in the direction of one of the hallways, before looking back down at his cards. "Don't take too long."

"Of course," I reply curtly as I stand up and head in the direction he nodded towards. Once I'm out of his eyesight, I cut back across the back of the room, careful to stay out of his view, and slip a small keycard out of my pocket. I smile to myself as it scans and flashes green, granting me access to a separate area of private rooms I remember all too well from my childhood. Silently, I thank the sick fuck whose card I stole after I tracked her down recently. Her body is currently decomposing in the cement of a recently constructed building downtown. She's just one of the many on my list to dispose of and it's been a long time coming.

I make my way down a few hallways before entering a familiar door. Pop music assaults my ears. It's not dark and sultry like other areas of The Cellar. It's light and fun sounding. It's childish and it's fucking disgusting. I stop and grab a pill that looks identical to a candy heart from a bowl to my right that a small woman with pigtails holds, before making my way to a couch and sitting down. I pocket the pill, not bothering to pretend to swallow it when I realize no one has paid me any attention. The room is full of sick fucks who have all downed at least one of these pills by now. They dance and gyrate against each other while waiting for their number to be announced. They are all sweaty, pupils fully dilated, and unaware of the danger sitting right in front of them.

I can't wait to set this place on fire and watch them all burn, but for now, only one man will have to satisfy my craving. I hear his voice before I see him. He sits on a couch, surrounded by other men and women. His large stomach bounces grotesquely while he laughs, no doubt telling some ridiculous story to the imbeciles who surround him. Igor Fanz is a regular in The Cellar. Both Jonathan and I figured that out fairly quickly once we became of age to attend events. He shifts off of the couch and I watch him walk through a doorway before I smoothly stand and proceed to follow. I remember this area leading to a large bathroom area set up much like a locker room. This would be a clean up area for guests. A smaller duplicate one, mirrors the one I'm in, just on the other side of the main room. That one is for the entertainment. My nose wrinkles when I step around a corner and see Igor drop his clothes before stepping into a small private steam room they call a torch room. I quickly catch the door with my foot before it has the chance to lock me out and enter behind him. He spins around, noting my cloak and hood still on and narrows his eyes.

"This is a private room," he says assertively, as I glance around at the various large pots of boiling water emitting steam throughout the room.

I don't say anything, as I step forward and remove my hood. I see his throat muscles work as he assesses me. It's clear he realizes the danger he's in, but has no idea why.

"Hello, Igor," I purr out as I advance on him and grab him by the throat. I slam his body down on the bench, causing him to cry out in pain. These rooms are all sound proof. Everything in The Cellar is sound proof. I relish that fact as I whip out my pocket knife and slash down his cheek. He howls in pain and proceeds to cover the wound, but it's deep and the blood oozes between his fingers.

"Who…who are you?" He asks me. "What do you want?"

I grin manically at him and repeat the set of words he spoke every single time he took my brother from me. "I get off imagining the twin bond is real. That you will feel every beautiful thing that happens."

His eyes widen at my words, and he attempts to stand and push past me, but he's too slow. My knife slams into his stomach and I lean in closely, before whispering his ear. "It's only fair Igor…that he gets to feel every beautiful thing I do to you. After all," I say as I drag the knife across his stomach and his intestines slide out, "we are twins and we are very much bonded."

Igor's body falls to the bench and slumps over as he bleeds out in front of me. His glassy eyes begin to fade far too quickly for my liking. I would have quite liked to take my time with him, but I'm currently running out of it. I wouldn't be surprised if Antonio hasn't already noticed me missing. Not wasting a second, I haul the large pot of boiling water off its stand and tip it over Igor's body. I watch entranced, as his skin turns red and begins to blister. I smile when I hear his low, agonizing moans. The sound of my whistling fills the room as I proceed to tip the remaining pots of water over his body and exit. I rinse and wipe my bloody hands before quickly heading back the way I originally entered. Hopefully they don't find his body until after we have already left.

Chapter 21

Kaz

    I've just finished my last file for the day and I decide to head up to Jonathan and Jamison's office floor. Apparently, I'm still being babysat because of the whole Lockhart debacle. I roll my eyes as I step off the elevator. If these guys only knew how easily I can handle myself. I don't need anyone to watch me. I stop short when I hear what sounds like an argument coming from the meeting room. Peering around the corner, I can just make out Jamison's back while he sits in a chair. Jonathan paces in front of the door, making me shrink back further. The last thing I need is to be caught eavesdropping.

    "His wife is on television, Jamison. She's fucking crying about him missing."

    Jamison laughs and the sound is so foreign it makes me wrinkle my nose. "And?" He asks Jonathan. I can't see his face, but his tone is all kinds of amused.

    "I can't lose you," he says while running his hands through his hair. "What if you were caught? What if...what if..." His words die off and he almost sounds choked up. Jamison stands and immediately wraps his arms around Jonathan in an embrace. What the fuck is going on? I'm thoroughly weirded out by seeing this side of Jamison. A pang of jealousy hits me. Is that what it's like when Jamison cares about you? I was convinced he didn't have any feelings at all, but watching this encounter with his brother is changing my entire perception of him. Seeing them like this is fucking with my head. What would it be like to be a part of that? I'm sure the many women they have fucked together would tell me it was fantastic, but I don't want to know about just the sex, I want to know what it would be like to be part of that emotional connection they share. I bite my lip before shaking my head. What a stupid thought. The most I could ever hope for would be great sex and I'm not sure I would actually have the balls to do that with both of them anyway. I may not be innocent in that department, but that is certainly way past my area of expertise. How would that work, anyway? I rub my thighs together to relieve the friction before mentally slapping myself. Enough of that shit, Kaz. Get it the fuck together. My eyes squeeze shut as I lean against the wall collecting my thoughts and when I open them again, prepared to push off and round the corner, I'm greeted with two sets of blue ones. Jamison's look deep and angry while Jonathan's are bright and worried.

"Are you okay, Kaz?" Jonathan asks me as he grabs my arm and pulls me off the wall. I didn't realize how much I was leaning against it until I'm actually standing up straight, staring up at both men.

"I didn't realize eavesdropping was in your job description, Kitten," Jamison accuses while watching me with an annoyed expression.

I don't have a chance to defend myself because Jonathan jumps to my rescue.

"Shut up, Jamison." They both glare at each other before I catch a quick glimpse of Jamison's eyes softening.

He rolls his eyes before replying, "Fine, we can discuss what is in the job description of the head of HR another time. We should figure out food before heading back to the apartment for the weekend."

My head whips around. "The weekend? I didn't realize this was a fucking sleepover. I didn't pack anything and I'm really not sure this is the best idea." I grab the ruffles on my blouse and nervously twist my fingers around them.

"I have acquired the correct items for you. Everything you need will be there," Jamison replies.

I huff out loud and cross my arms. "You don't know what

I need."

"You aren't afraid to spend the night in our apartment, are you?" He asks me with a devious glint in his eye. I know he's fricking baiting me and the truth is, yeah, I'm scared. I'm nervous as fuck. I've slept with both of these men and I'm not sure I can handle spending an entire weekend alone with both of them together. There's a giant elephant in the room right now and it's waiting for someone to let it out.

"I'm going to need a drink to deal with your guys' fighting this whole weekend. Let's hit a dive bar," Jonathan interrupts with a smile.

"Fantastic," Jamison deadpans before heading to the elevator.

Thirty minutes later, we are sitting at a table top bar slamming down our second shot. Well, Jonathan and I are. Jamison is sitting there with his phone in hand and one foot casually on his knee. Does he ever put his phone down? The alcohol has me buzzing pretty fast and feeling pretty ballsy.

"Find any good porn sites on that thing?" I ask nonchalantly, attempting a jab at Jamison.

He places his phone face down before placing his hands under his chin and leaning on them. "Define good? Tell me, Kitten, what do you search for? Maybe you're into role playing? A student who hides under her professor's desk, pleasuring him while he teaches a class? Or possibly a little anal action…"

His words are interrupted by the sound of me choking on the cocktail I was sipping. Jonathan smacks my back lightly, before looking at me with concern. "Everything okay?"

"Yes," I say, while shooting daggers with my eyes at his brother. The fucking asshole just smirks at me. It's then that my phone buzzes on the small table in front of us. The screen lights up with a notification of an incoming text from Riley, probably laughing at the message I sent her earlier, telling her I'll never forgive her for leaving me alone with these two. Jamison snatches my phone up and glares at the screen.

"What the fuck is wrong with you? Give me my damn

phone," I yell, while he holds it out of reach.

"Jesus, Jamison. Give her her phone back. People are starting to stare."

Jamison ignores his brother and leans in close as he shows me the front screen.

"Who the fuck is that?" He growls out as he points at the photo of my missing childhood best friend and I. I have a momentary feeling of sadness before it's replaced by anger. The nerve of him.

"That," I say, pointing to the phone screen, "Is my best friend from childhood who went missing years ago."

He stares at me like he's waiting for me to explain further.

"You are a real piece of work. How dare you look at my phone. You have no right!"

I swipe my phone from his hand quickly, before he has a chance to pull it away from me again, and stand from my chair abruptly. "I'm ready to leave now," I grit out before I slam down the rest of my cocktail and turn around, heading for the exit. I can hear them both bickering behind me, but I don't care to listen. I'm so mad right now, I'm practically seeing red. The ride to their apartment is spent in complete silence. It's only when we make it back there and Jamison attempts to give orders that all hell breaks loose.

'Don't tell me what to fucking do, Jamison!" I yell out with both hands on my hips.

He gets in my face angrily. "I was not telling you what to do. I was simply informing you of where the stuff I purchased was and how the sleeping arrangements would be most suitable. You are insufferable."

"You are an asshole!" I say, glaring at him around Jonathan as he attempts to push us apart. "I'm not a child. I'm a grown ass woman and I can do whatever the fuck I want." Before I even realize what I'm doing I have Jonathan's shirt in my hands and I'm ripping him down to me and crashing my lips against him. I know I've caught him by surprise when he doesn't immediately respond to my advances, so I lick into the seam of his lips. His mouth opens for me and he swipes his tongue out and tangles it with mine as he grabs me around the waist and pulls me into him. I can feel him harden against my stomach as I press my body against his. I pull away enough to see his eyes open wide.

"What was that for?" he asks me bewildered.

I still have my hands gripping his shirt as I peer over at Jamison, expecting to see anger in his eyes. Instead, I'm assaulted by his lustful gaze. He's looking at me like he wants to devour me. I'm suddenly a bit nervous. I think I just opened a can of worms and I'm not sure the lid will fit back on by the time this night ends.

"Do it again," Jamison's voice rasps out.

"What?" I ask him, confused. Does he want me to kiss Jonathan again in front of him? I look at Jonathan questioningly, but he cups my jaw and leans in to kiss me again before I can react. He pulls me toward him just as the feel of another body envelopes me from behind. I feel Jamison's hand push my hair over my shoulder before his mouth connects with my neck. My whole body stiffens and Jonathan's hand squeezes my hip hard. My eyes shoot open and he pulls back the tiniest bit before murmuring. "Is this okay?"

Jamison's hand is wrapped around the back of my neck while he grazes his teeth against me. I'm so turned on I can't think straight. Is this really happening and is it okay? I'm not even sure, honestly. I don't know how I'll feel tomorrow, but right now, I'm on fucking fire. I nod my head yes, just slightly, and I know I've said the right thing when the tension from Jonathan drops and he smiles, visibly relieved. The sound of my zipper opening breaks the silence and I bite my lip when Jonathan's eyes glitter. He helps Jamison pull my dress from my shoulders and it pools at my feet, revealing my deep red lace bra and panty set and the strap where my dagger sits wrapped around my thigh. He eyes the dagger but doesn't comment on it. Instead, he pulls his shirt over his head in one swift motion, showing off every delicious curve of his muscles. My gaze trails down his chest and abs before settling on the perfectly cut "v" with the small trail of hair that leads below his pants. My hands eagerly reach for the button on his pants to undo them.

"Look at you, Kitten, so eager to please," Jamison whispers as he nibbles my ear lobe. I lean into him, moaning. Jonathan's pants drop, leaving him in only a pair of silky black boxer briefs. He grabs me and picks me up and my legs immediately wrap around his torso as he carries me to his bedroom. I have the perfect view of Jamison unbuttoning his shirt as he trails behind us, watching our every move. My mouth waters as I watch him remove his shirt and pants to reveal an entirely inked body underneath. His muscles ripple, showing off every intricate design inked on him. My view is cut off by the sudden drop when Jonathan twists his body to fall flat on his back on his bed, making me straddle his waist in the process. His very hard length presses against my core, making me wiggle in anticipation as he grinds up against me.

"Fuck, I can feel how wet you are through my boxers," Jonathan groans out as Jamison's hands glide down my body from behind. He's so fast I don't realize he's removed my dagger and sliced through my panties until he already has it placed back in its sheath. He removes my bra quickly, before pinching my nipples, sending electricity straight to my core and making me gasp out in surprise.

Jonathan eyes me with a smirk before grabbing me by my ass and hauling my body directly up to his face. He grins from below as I look down at him with a flush in my cheeks. "Don't act shy now, Pretty Girl. We've been in this position before."

I flush again before looking back over my shoulder to see Jamison completely naked and eyeing me hungrily. "Yeah, well usually there isn't someone watching us either."

Jamison's eyes glitter. "Oh I don't plan to just watch, Kitten. I fully intend to participate," he says as he stalks around the bed and climbs up on it. His dick juts out right in front of my face and he takes my jaw in his hand and guides me toward it. "Be a good girl and keep your mouth full while Jonathan makes sure you're nice and wet for us."

"She's dripping already," Jonathan groans before yanking me down onto his face. I cry out in shock as his mouth connects with my pussy and he immediately slides his tongue inside me. My moans are muffled, when Jamison shoves his cock inside my mouth, hitting the back of my throat. I can't think straight as he ruthlessly fucks my face while Jonathan's mouth devours me from below. All of my senses are completely overloaded. The feel of Jonathan's fingers inside me and his mouth sucking on my clit send me over the edge and I moan out around Jamison's dick as I come undone. He pulls from my mouth, running his thumb along my bottom lip while looking at me with...I'm not sure? Maybe adoration? If that's even possible for him.

"Fuck, Kitten, you look so fucking sexy when you come apart like that."

His words surprise me. He doesn't normally compliment and I'm not sure how to take it. In any case, I don't have time to evaluate his words as Jonathan grabs my hips and pulls me down towards his very erect dick and lifts me above him. He must have already removed his boxers because he's now completely naked. He slides me down inch by inch slowly, like he's savoring the way it feels.

"I love how tight and wet you are for me, Pretty Girl," he groans out while he bites his bottom lip. "But fuck, you are extra wet tonight."

"Tell him, Kitten," Jamison's voice whispers in my ear from behind me suddenly. He pushes me down so I'm hovering above Jonathan, looking him directly in the eyes. "Tell my brother what a little slut you are."

I look at Jonathan as he pumps himself leisurely in and out of me from below. He doesn't look mad or jealous. The feel of slick lube pours down my ass crack and my eyes go wide as Jamison's finger enters me from behind.

"Are you?" Jonathan asks, grabbing my jaw as I push back against Jamison's now two fingers and I moan out uncontrollably. He squeezes, forcing my eyes open wide. I shake my head no as Jamison's fingers pull out of me, leaving me wanting more.

He leans over my body and bites into my shoulder hard. I cry out in surprise. "Don't fucking lie, Kitten. Show him what a good little slut you are. Only for us, though, right?" He notches the head of his dick against my ass and presses himself inside the smallest fraction, groaning out from behind me and squeezing my hips hard with both hands.

Jonathan stills below me. "Only for us, Pretty Girl?" he says, as he cups my jaw and leans up to kiss me. I'm at a loss for words, so I nod yes because I think I am. I will be whatever the hell these two want at this moment.

Jamison presses further inside me. "Fuck, you are so fucking tight," I whine out and wriggle. I don't know if I'm dying to stay or trying to get away.

"You're doing so good, Pretty Girl. Look how well you are taking us both." Jonathan whispers as he kisses me passionately.

"She's barely fucking taking me. Don't start praising her yet, brother," Jamison grits out as he grabs my hair at the nape of my neck, holding me still while he pushes himself further inside.

Jonathan's thumb swipes across my clit, sending a jolt through my body. "Fuck, fuck," I whimper as he continues to rub me and I push back into Jamison, causing him to groan in surprise when he is fully seated inside me. He pulls me up toward him and wraps his hand around my neck, causing me to arch my back while he licks along my neck and plays with my nipple. Jonathan begins to pump in and out of me from below while still rubbing my clit. I don't know what I'm even saying, but the sounds coming from my mouth cannot be anything more than mumbled nonsense. I'm complete putty in between both of these men. I can't even think straight as Jamison pushes me back down on my hands and pumps himself inside me along with his brother. I don't know what to do. I'm just along for the ride as my orgasm slams into me and I come around both men, clamping down hard. I cry out so loud, I'm sure the neighbors ten stories below can probably hear me.

"Holy shit," Jonathan swears as he slams up inside me, filling me to the brim.

Jamison pumps furiously behind me and wraps his hand around to play with my already sensitive clit. "Be a good girl and come again for us. One more time baby, so we can feel you clamp down on us while we fill your ass and pussy with our cum."

My eyes whip open. Not because of his dirty words, but because he just called me baby. I look down to see Jonathan smirking. "You heard my brother, Pretty Girl. Come for us." At his words, I shatter between the both of them. I come so fucking hard, I almost black out. Both men pump and groan in unison as their orgasms rip through them and they slam inside me before stilling. I fall onto Jonathan while Jamison leans over me, breathing hard. That was fucking incredible. I mean sex was good with just one of them, but both of them, together, that was on another level entirely. They gently pull out, causing me to whimper at the loss of the feeling of having them both so close. I move to lay on my side next to Jonathan as he turns and peppers kisses along my face and jaw. "You're so fucking perfect, Pretty Girl."

Jamison leans over me as he picks me up bridal style. "He's right, Kitten. You belong to us now."

I'm so worn out I can't even speak, so I just nod yes in agreement as I'm taken into the bathroom, where both men proceed to clean me up and pamper me. If this is a dream, I don't ever want to wake up…

Chapter 22

Jamison

Two weeks later

I'm back at The Cellar, this time left to my own devices, and I'm not even mad about it. Not one bit. After my brother and I spent our weekend fucking Kaz, we attempted to act normal at work for the next week. We had all made a deal. It lasted about four hours into Monday before I walked into Kaz's office where I found Jonathan on his knees licking Kaz's sweet pussy while she was splayed across her fucking desk like a Thanksgiving turkey. The door had been locked, but little did she know, I had an extra key made for her office years ago. I promptly fucked her face in punishment while she came all over Jonathan's tongue before walking out of her office and slamming the door behind me. I've tried to keep my distance, at least while around the other men of Bolt Corporation, but I'm fairly certain they're all aware something is going on. Sebastian had mentioned wanting to discuss something with me but Xavier was drugged and kidnapped last weekend so we haven't had the chance to converse properly. I've avoided him all week in hopes that this entire Sasha and Lockhart situation will distract him from what I know he is probably wanting to discuss. I haven't touched Kaz in three days and I'm already feeling slightly unhinged. After having her fully with Jonathan two weeks ago...The way she took us both so fucking well. How fucking perfect she looked when she came apart with us. I can't even think about anyone else.

I open and close the lighter in my pocket while standing

against the wall in the back of the main casino room of The Cellar. Apparently, after our last visit, they must have realized they needed to up security so I won't be entering through the back door again unfortunately. There are now two guards there and neither looks to be leaving anytime soon. No matter though, after all, I'm only here for a distraction. I'll be damned if I don't make it a worthwhile one though. I make my way towards the doorway Xavier and Andre entered through a few minutes before. The guard eyes me but says nothing as I walk past him, whistling and smiling at him manically. He's probably so used to the sick fucking perverts that come here, it doesn't even faze him anymore. A few twists and turns and I come to a stop in front of a door with the signature Triad triangle above it. Ahh, the Gluttony room. What better way to cause a little distraction than to do it in a room full of ridiculously entitled pricks. I enter the room like a complete and utter asshole, my head held high like I own the place. Heads swivel in my direction and I smile wide, my face painting, I'm sure is throwing everyone off. The room is dimmed in low blue lighting. Tables throughout the room are covered in all types of food, including large baskets of fruit. I pop a few grapes in my mouth and wiggle my fingers at a few onlookers, making them smile and nod. Idiots. People lounge all around the large room on couches and cushions with pets close by. By pet, I mean a collared slave. I pat the head of one currently on his knees next to a man as I slide past him to sit on an available couch.

"You like to watch or do you plan to choose someone?" The man asks me curiously before motioning his head towards a large cage on a stage in the corner of the room. I eye the cage before turning back towards him.

"I'll see where the night takes me." My eyes flick to his slave who is currently bowed, head down. He raises his eyes to peer up at me before quickly lowering them again when he sees I'm watching him. I squint, racking my brain. Why does this man look familiar? The man sitting on the couch laughs and makes some joke about me sharing his slave, but I barely hear him. The slave's eyes lift to mine again and that's when it hits me. I whip my phone out quickly when I feel it vibrate in my pants. Fuck. I tap into my app and press a few buttons. The lights go out a moment later, causing everyone around to freak out.

"What do you think is going on?" The man on the couch yells over the commotion.

"I'm not sure," I reply to him, still staring at his slave when the lights flicker back on. The slave hasn't left his position and his eyes are still trained on me. With record speed, I swipe into another app full of photos and screenshots, before finding the picture I'm looking for. A devilish smirk appears on my face. Well, well, well. Imagine my motherfucking luck. If I was gambling tonight, I would have hit the jackpot. A text comes through and I read it before swiping back to my previous app and pressing a few buttons again. I raise my eyes, the smile still on my face as I stare at the slave and he watches me back. Fear crosses his features before the room goes dark again.

"I'm going to find out what's going on." The man on the couch says before standing unsteadily and stumbling past the slave. I don't have time to explain anything to him. I have somewhere to be, so I whip out the keycard I have and a one-hundred dollar bill, before dropping to my knees and grabbing the slave by his collar to yank him closer. His whole body freezes in fear when he feels my hand shove into his small briefs. I can tell he's relieved when I pull my hand out just as quickly.

"There's a keycard in there that unlocks everything to this place. I believe you have a friend who would love to see you. Unfortunately, this is all the help I can offer you, but if you make it out of here alive, remember the name Bolt Corporation." I yank him closer. "If you get caught and utter one word of this to anyone in here, I will make sure this collar is the least of your worries. I know for certain, there are rooms far worse than this one."

The lights flick back on just as I'm standing up and sliding out another door. I make it out to the main room just in time to see Andre wrap his arms around two guards, swaying slightly.

Fuck, that was close. Well, looks like I'll have to improvise a bit, I think as I pull a cigarette from someone's pack on a close-by table and light it up, before inhaling deeply. Fuck, that's good. I haven't had one of these in a while. I grab two drinks off a server's tray and twist around to say thank you as they scowl at me. My body hits one of the guards and one of my drinks splashes all over him. Oopsie.

"What the fuck?" The guard screams at me.

He smacks the other drink out of my hand, causing it to spill all over the floor and curtain nearby.

"There's no smoking in the lobby," he seethes out while I contemplate stubbing my cigarette out in his eye. I would really like to press it down and find out how deep of a hole it would burn before it went out completely, but I'll settle for watching his whole body go up in flames instead.

"That was costly liquor you wasted," I reply, before dropping my lit cigarette at his feet.

He screams as his leg erupts in flames. I see Andre yank Xavier away out of my peripheral vision, and for a moment, I stand and enjoy the scene around me. Complete chaos ensues as the tablecloth and curtains around us also erupt in flames. I hope this whole fucking place burns to the ground. Unfortunately, I know that one cigarette will never be enough to make that happen. Without a second thought, I turn and push through the crowd, leaving the burning guard to scream out in agony as he rolls on the ground. I smile at the text I receive from Andre, letting me know everything went as planned. 'Hopefully, more than just Sasha made it out tonight," I think, remembering the slave from earlier and the fear in his eyes.

Chapter 23

Jonathan

One Week Later

"How's the new live in? You think you'll add her to your harem of future wives?" I can barely contain my laughter as I joke with Andre. He snorts, clearly annoyed with me already.

"Fuck off, Jonathan. What did you call me for anyway?"

"Well," I answer him as I casually stick my feet up on top of my desk as I lean back in my chair. "I was calling to let you know how Xavier's meeting with his dearest uncle Lockhart went. He looked over the contract and actually signed it. Xavier is now the proud owner of Lock & Key."

Andre whistles over the line. "Damn, that's great. I can't believe he went for it."

"You want to know the best part?" I ask him, enthusiastically.

"I'm betting you're going to tell me even if I say no," Andre laughs.

"He agreed to leave Sasha alone."

The line is silent. Thirty seconds go by before I look at my screen to make sure we haven't been disconnected. "Hello, Andre? You there?"

"Uh, yeah. I'm here," he replies.

What the heck is this guy's problem? You would think he would be more excited about this news. He didn't seem too happy to be babysitting Sasha anyway. If Lockhart has agreed to leave her alone, that means she can come back. Andre would be off the hook.

"Andre, man I really thought there would be a little more excitement from you right now. I mean hello, Sasha won't have to be in your hair anymore and you can get back to doing whatever the hell eligible mafia bachelors do these days." I laugh at my own joke before realizing Andre is still silent. "Andre?"

He sighs loudly into the phone. "I don't think it's a good idea for her to come back yet."

I set the phone down on my desk and put it on speaker as I pull my legs off and settle them on the ground. Leaning over the phone, I stare at his contact name, a bit confused. "Are you trying to play a joke on me?"

"No Jonathan. No joking. Think about it. I don't trust Lockhart. Why would he give up Sasha so easily like that?"

I ponder what he says for a second. He's not wrong. Lockhart is conniving and skeezy. We still don't have any clue who this mysterious son is. For all we know, he could be anyone close to us. "Well, I mean, I guess I can talk to Xavier. All jokes aside, is Sasha doing okay out there?"

"That woman," Andre grits out in frustration. "She's fine. I can handle her out here for a bit longer. I'll speak to Xavier."

Just then, Xavier enters my office, whistling. There's a clear show of happiness on his face. He's been through so much, it's about time he got his happy ending.

"Xavier just walked in. I can fill him in," I say as a crash sounds on Andre's end.

"What the fuck?" Andre yells. "Fucking scocciatura." Another crash sounds and we can hear women arguing in the background. Andre must have left his phone wherever he was because he sounds far away. "Listen, Princess," is all we hear before there is a ton of mumbling. He finally gets back on the phone, sounding thoroughly irritated.

"I have to go. Tell Xavier I'll speak with him later."

Xavier and I both bust out laughing when the line goes dead.

"What was that all about?" He asks me.

"Well," I smile, barely able to hide my enjoyment. "Andre

was just informing me about how he thought it better to keep Sasha there a little longer, just in case Lockhart decides to not uphold his end of the deal. I have a feeling whatever was going on is giving him second thoughts."

Xavier smirks. "I'm honestly more worried about Andre than Sasha at this point. I know she will be safe with him. I'm not sure he will be safe from her, however. Maybe it's time a woman gives him a run for his money instead of dropping to his feet in hopes of becoming his bride."

"Fuck if that ain't the truth. His daddy has been waiting to marry him off for so long now, I'm honestly surprised it's taking so long. What could possibly be so important that he hasn't found one he likes yet?"

"Did you forget how picky his dad is? Who knows what weird shit he makes those women do before sending them to Andre." Xavier looks at me with disgust. We both visibly shutter. I can't imagine my father, if I had one, picking my future wife for me. Then again, I can't imagine anyone besides my Pretty Girl becoming my wife, anyway.

"I'm surprising Corrine this weekend with Lock & Key," Xavier says, drawing me from my thoughts. Thank god too because I almost went down the rabbit hole imagining Kaz naked underneath me and all of the things I want to do to her. I really don't need to be sporting a raging hard on right now while Xavier is in my office.

"Sounds like fun," I reply as I discreetly adjust myself.

Xavier catches on and notices what I'm doing. "I'm going to leave you to take care of whatever is going on down there. I just wanted to let you know not to make any plans for the weekend. I want everyone there for the big reveal. It needs to be epic for my Butterfly."

I roll my eyes before motioning for him to leave with my hand. "Yeah, yeah I'll be there, okay. Now get out of here. I have work to do."

He laughs as he leaves and I pick my phone back up, fully prepared to send a naughty message to Kaz so I can play out the dirty scenario I started in my head.

Chapter 24

Kaz
Present Day

I make my way out of the VIP section and down the stairs quietly. I've had at least six shots and numerous drinks already tonight, and I'm feeling a bit too tipsy. Besides that, I can't take any more innuendoes from Jonathan. My phone chimes from my purse, and I roll my eyes. That's probably him now, asking where I went.

"None of your fucking business," I mumble to myself as I stumble down the last few stairs. I attempt to lean up against the wall when a strong hand grips me around my neck, pulling me behind a curtain.

"You are my fucking business," a deep voice growls out as I'm pushed up against a wall. I look up, startled but relax when I realize who has me in a chokehold. Deep blue eyes glare down at me. I would know those eyes anywhere.

Jamison presses in close, and I catch myself arching against him, causing him to smirk. Bastard. His hair is perfectly gelled back, and he wears his signature suit, which covers every delicious part of his body. "What are you doing wandering around by yourself?" he asks me, tilting his head to the side like a fucking psychopath.

"I'm leaving."

"By yourself," he states like it wasn't obvious.

I swat his hand off my neck, in an attempt to get the feel of him off me. I'm already tipsy. I don't need to give my body any more incentive to betray me more than it already has. My skin is already flushed and hot. I'm mentally trying to will myself to cool down.

"What's wrong, Kitten?" he asks with a smirk.

"I've already told you a million times to stop calling me that," I say as I try to move around him. He blocks my path before crossing his arms.

"You cannot leave by yourself. It's still not completely safe. Why didn't you ask Jonathan to take you?"

"I didn't feel like it, okay?" I say, mimicking him by crossing my arms.

He glares at me before grabbing my arm. "Let's go, I'll take you home."

"I don't need you to chauffeur me everywhere, Jamison." I yank my arm from him, and the room tilts briefly. I fall back onto the stairs behind me.

He stands above me, crossing his arms again. "Why do you have to be so disobedient?"

"You're not my boss. I mean, you're not my boss. I, I…" My words trail off, and he raises his brow at me. I'm way too fucking drunk for this, I think to myself before an idea comes over me. Pushing out my bottom lip, I look up sadly at him.

"Fine, take me home," I say as I pretend to search for something in my purse. "I think I left my keys on the table in the corner upstairs."

"I will go get them. Stay put," he says as he pushes past me.

I bolt out of the stairway and quickly leave as soon as he opens the door.

"Sucker," I say, laughing out loud. I'm not in any shape to drive, and no drivers are currently outside the club. I don't plan to wait for one to show up, either. I need to get the hell away from both of the twins before I do something stupid.

It wouldn't be the first time I've gotten tipsy and let my inhibitions go. I roll my eyes at my idiocy as I quickly make my way down another street and notice a cab pull up beside me. A large, good-looking man sits in the driver's seat, motioning for me to jump into the passenger's seat. It's not normal for a cab driver, but I need a ride and I'm fresh out of options. For all I know, Jamison is already outside looking for me. I jump in and click my seat belt as he drives away.

"Where to, babe?" the guy asks. Something about the way he says it sets me on high alert. My hand moves discreetly towards the small knife I have strapped to my inner thigh under my dress. Call it intuition or whatever you want. This man's demeanor does not scream friendly cab driver. I look at him warily as he glances at me quickly before speeding up.

"Don't even think about jumping out," he says when he notices me eyeballing the door. "I have a proposition for you, Little Devil."

I close my eyes briefly and try to calm my nerves. I haven't heard that nickname in a very long time. "Who's asking?" I ask calmly.

"My boss. He wanted me to let you know he would be in touch."

"Why the hell did he send you?" I ask, perplexed.

"I was heading in this direction anyway. I have a flight to catch." He moves his hand over the center console towards me as he pulls the car over to the side of the road where there aren't any lights. "I have a few minutes, though, and I heard you put up a good fight. Why don't you show me why they call you Little Devil?"

"My pleasure," I purr and flutter my eyelashes, leaning towards him. The sound of his scream echoes inside the car as I stab my knife through his hand, impaling it on the console.

"You fucking bitch," he screams as I whip the door open and scramble out of the car.

"Tell your boss to fuck off," I yell back at him as I make my way around a corner and back onto a well-lit street. I spot a small diner and quickly search for a booth before pulling out my phone.

I dial the number, annoyed at myself and my current situation.

"Hello, Kitten," Jamison answers.
"Come pick me up. I'll send you the address."
"I knew you would change your mind."
"Whatever," I say as I hang up.

I look down at my phone to see a new notification on it. Pulling up my messages, I find one from an unknown number.

Hello, Little Devil. It seems you are a hard person to get in touch with. Let me make this easy for you. You will give me the information I need or I will inform Bolt Corporation that not only have they hired a fraud, they also have employed someone who was actively known in the underground.

I grit my teeth together as I read the message before responding.

Who the fuck is this and what do you want?

Three dots appear quickly before another text message.

You can start with following Jamison. I want to know where he disappears to every Wednesday evening. I also require something else. I'll text you for that later. Don't open your mouth, Little Devil. What would your boss have to say if he found out just how deep you used to be? Would any of them want you close to their wives or girlfriends, knowing the danger you could put them in?

Rage pours through my body. I don't like being threatened or blackmailed. God knows how long I've had to deal with Jamison. But with him, it just hits differently. Maybe it's the attraction between us that's always been there? Or, I don't know, the way I have always been pretty sure he wasn't ever going to spill my secrets. I could be wrong of course, but either way, this feels different. This feels worse, more dangerous, and suddenly I'm scared. I'm scared for my friends and the guys. Scared that the life I was trying to escape has come back for me, and this time when it crumbles to the ground, it's going to drag me all the way down with it. My fingers move of their own accord as I type out my response quickly.

Understood.

The anonymous texter's response comes through so quickly this time, I would swear he already had it typed and ready to send.

That's the good Little Devil, I've heard all about. I'll be in touch.

My teeth grit together and I slam my phone on the diner table as Jamison strolls in.
"What is going on?" he asks me questioningly.
"Nothing," I grit out as I slide out of the booth and past him, walking towards the doors. "Just take me home."
He doesn't respond. I'm sure he can tell I'm in no mood tonight. Instead, he walks me out to the curb and holds the door to his car open for me before slipping into the driver's side and driving me home, where I know I'm going to spend the rest of the night unable to sleep. How the hell am I supposed to follow someone who always seems to be watching everyone else? And what the hell else could I possibly do for this anonymous person without getting caught. At this point, I might be in a lose, lose situation and that, well, it's scary as fuck.

Chapter 25

Lockhart

"Are you fucking kidding me?" I scream at my desk as I stand hunched over it, staring at my phone screen. Devin's face is visible, but he's not looking directly at me. He's got me propped up on the counter of some shitty bathroom while he re-wraps his hand. I can see the wound that that little bitch inflicted on him is still bleeding from both sides of his hand. A nicer man would care. I'm not a nicer man. He's sweating profusely, probably from the pain. Fucking pussy. How can someone who enjoys inflicting pain on others be such a goddamn little bitch.

He turns to me after shoving a couple pills in his mouth and grabs his phone to hold it closer to his face. "I'm sorry, boss. I already have myself scheduled for the next flight out. I won't let you down again."

"Damn right you won't," I seethe into the phone. "I don't need another fuck up, Devin. Only the best will be at my side. Everyone else will be discarded like the rest of the trash."

"Understood," he replies, while looking directly at me. That's what I like about Devin. He knows his place and he's eager to keep it. I won't trust anyone ever fully, but he's as close as they get. I hang up the phone without saying goodbye and breathe out a heavy sigh. Movement on the floor to my left catches my eye.

"It's okay," I say, petting the head of the cowering man curled up on his knees, looking at the floor. He's completely naked and collared, the hard ridges of his body fully on display for me. His body quakes with fear, making me smile. "Daddy isn't mad at you."

My phone rings again, dragging my face from my pet.

"A little birdie told me you made a deal recently. A deal involving a club that I was also utilizing," the voice says smoothly when I answer the call.

I smirk. "It served a purpose."

"Did it now?" he asks. I can tell it's more of a statement and not so much of a question, but we have been sharing small pieces of information for quite some time now, so no harm in letting on a little more.

"It did," I reply. "I needed Xavier off my back. He signed everything over to me." I can't help the triumph I feel over that statement.

He chuckles, "Ahh, the infamous nephew. Whatever will you do without an heir?"

"I don't need a fucking heir. I don't need anyone trying to usurp me." I grit my teeth together to control my temper. He doesn't know that I might, in fact, have an heir. One I knew nothing about until recently when DNA papers mysteriously showed up in an envelope to my office. Of course they could have been fake, but I can't take any chances. I need to know for one hundred percent certainty.

"Someone else will try to take you out and if they succeed..." he voices, cutting into my thoughts.

"You let me worry about that. It doesn't concern you."

"It concerns me when it begins to affect the business... and The Triad," he says, angrily. "Slaves keep ending up missing and it all leads back to us. It's only a matter of time before we have more than just the third breathing down our neck."

"I know," I sigh out in frustration. "I'm taking care of my end, so how about you worry about yours for now, especially considering our issues have been commingled."

"Excuse me?" He asks. The annoyance in his voice is evident.

"Oh yes, you didn't know yet?" I snicker. "Well, I look forward to your phone call after you pay your precious heir a little visit. And just so we are clear, I expect a return on my investment. I'm sending someone to collect for me soon." My finger clicks end call and I lean back in my chair sighing in clear frustration. I can feel my control slowly slipping. Years of making sure everything worked in my favor. Years of me executing the perfect plan, slowly collecting all of my pieces, and carefully placing them where they need to be. Now it could all end with one fucking file, that it seems, has created twice as many problems. I stare at the file with disgust, my past memories rushing to the forefront of my mind.

The little vixen who hung around my brother and all of his friends. She was a sexy little thing, only a few years younger than me. I knew the minute I saw her I had wanted her, even if she had eyes for my brother. I could see it in the way she watched him, but he never returned the sentiment. He didn't see what was right in front of him and instead, chose to play the third wheel in his friend's love life instead. Idiot. It didn't take much to woo her away. A few nice gestures and she was putty in my hands. She was also a fucking tease, never letting me get too close. After a few months, I grew tired of her games, pretending she was innocent and dragging me along. So I did what any logical man would do, what my father had ingrained in me from birth.

"A man takes what he wants, son. He doesn't wait for it to fall into his lap," he had said.

So I did. I took that little vixen out to the middle of the woods, promises of a picnic under the stars, and I stole from her. I stole the innocence I never thought she had. I fucked her on a blanket under those stars, her hands held tightly above her head while she cried out for me to stop. I licked the tears from her cheeks, while forcing myself inside her tight virgin cunt, the feel of her breaking around me while I thrust myself inside her, coming harder than I ever had in my life. The sight of my dick, streaked with the blood of her innocence as I pulled from her, was one I will never forget. My cum, dripping from her sweet pussy, so satisfying while she curled in on herself and cried.

Only then did I realize my mistake. In my attempt to grasp what I had wanted so badly, I had forgotten the one thing I never had before. The condom. A matter for the morning, I remember thinking, before taking her again, and again, and again. The next morning I was dropping her off down the street from her home, my cum, no doubt dried between her thighs. I had quickly acquired a small pill from the family doctor that same morning and I placed it into her hands, reminding her to not speak of the night's events to anyone ever.

"Say one word and I'll make sure your entire family disappears," I had said as I grasped her chin tightly. "You belong to me now."

She had left my car and I watched as she carefully slipped inside her home, attempting not to wake her parents. She tried to avoid me but she could never get too far. For months, I forced myself on her any way I could, whenever the opportunity arose and she never spoke a word to anyone. One day she just disappeared, not a trace to be found. Her family gone and the house left vacant. Eve...

Where the fuck is she now? I've scoured every file I could find. Hired countless private investigators, yet I still don't know what happened to her. She is the only explanation. The only time I was ever so stupid. Young and eager to take what had been teased and dangled in front of my face. I hadn't realized what the repercussions could be until now. Stupid of me to trust that girl to take the pill I had given to her. I should have forced it down her throat, followed by my dick. I should have made her swallow it down, chased by my cum. So. Fucking. Stupid. My father would be disgusted with me.

"Come here," I grit out as I yank the leash on my pet. He falls forward onto his hands and knees before quickly crawling to me. I pet his head, running my hands through his hair. "Be a good boy and take care of daddy."

Chapter 26

Jamison

    I watch Kaz as she walks down the street, casually looking over her shoulder every few seconds. To anyone else in this city, she is probably just some random girl nervous to be out past dark. I know better, though. My Kitten has claws just waiting to come out. From the corner of another building, I see her look around before entering a dingy looking bar. She looks nervous, but I'm unsure why. She can't see me, so I know I'm not the cause. Normally I wouldn't be following her around tonight seeing as how she's been following the same regiment for months now, however I've noticed she's been acting strange all week long. It started over the weekend when she had me pick her up after disappearing from the club. I wanted to fucking punish her for disobeying me so directly like that, especially considering the circumstances surrounding all of us at Bolt Corporation. I don't care what contracts were signed. I don't for one minute believe Lockhart gave up on Sasha so easily. Then, there is the matter of what he had said to me after his meeting with Xavier that day. I haven't stopped thinking about it since. It's almost as if he implied there was someone dangerous close to me. The devil herself. A woman. Kitten is the only woman I've let close to me and there's something off with her right now.

    I cross the street quickly and wait for a group of people to walk through the bar door. As soon as they begin piling in, I slide through, hoping to get lost in the small crowd. The inside of the bar is fucking filthy. My nose scrunches up at the distasteful decor scattered around. It looks like a bomb went off in a vintage secondhand store and they decided to take the remains and shove it all in here. I spot Kaz immediately in a booth, hunched over her phone. She's nervously tapping her fingers on the small table with her other hand. Thankfully, she isn't paying attention as I make my way past her and sit in another booth directly behind. The ugliest curtains hang between all of these booths, lightly knotted at the ends. They provide a somewhat detailed shield, but I pull the hoodie I stole from Jonathan up over my head and turn away, just in case. What the fuck is she doing here anyway? A server in a very skimpy outfit eyes me and starts heading my direction, so I wave her off with my hand while glaring like an asshole. She skitters away quickly, an annoyed look on her face. I'm two seconds away from sliding in Kaz's booth, my patience wearing thin, when a smooth voice makes my entire body freeze up.

"Hello, Little Devil," Lockhart purrs. "So nice to meet you face to face."

Kaz scoffs. "I should have known."

What should she have known? What the fuck is Lockhart doing meeting with her? My fingers close around the edge of the table hard, making my knuckles turn white as I continue listening.

"I believe you have something for me?" Lockhart asks her. It doesn't sound like a question, though. If anything, it's an assumption. I hear a rustling sound and Lockhart laughs.

"Your lap dog has something of mine as well, and I want it back." I hear Kaz grit out. She sounds angry. There isn't a trace of fear in her voice.

"Ahh, yes. He is currently out of the country right now on business. I'll have to see what we can do about that. You did quite the number on him, you know? I could use someone with your expertise, Little Devil. You could make lots of money. More than what Bolt Corporation pays you, I'm sure."

Something slams on the table and I hear Lockhart gasp. "You little bitch."

"I don't fight anymore. If you want to keep your fingers, I suggest you keep your hands on your side of the table. I brought you what you wanted. We are done here."

"Not so fast," Lockhart grits out. "We aren't done until I say we are."

I hear another rustling sound and see Kaz jolt up from the table and walk towards the exit, with Lockhart following close behind. He grabs her by the arm to stop her, but I can't hear anything else. Of course, the waitress from earlier thinks this is the perfect time to come over and ask me if I'm ready to order. By the time I've sent her on her way, Kaz and Lockhart are both gone.

"Fuck," I mutter, as I stand quickly and rush out of the bar, hoping I haven't lost them. Once I've made my way outside, I scan both sides of the street. A quick flash of Kaz's hair as she rounds a corner has me walking that direction. I know these streets like the back of my hand. She may be walking fast, but I know exactly where to go to cut her off. I cut through a back alley that curves over and connects with another street ahead. Once I reach the entrance of the alley, I stand and wait. Not thirty seconds pass before Kaz walks right next to the opening. I yank her into the dark, covering her mouth, and slam her against the brick wall. Her eyes go wide and her hands curl around my wrists, causing her nails to bite into my skin.

"Tell me, Kaz," I sneer as I lean right into her face and squeeze her neck with my other hand. "Are you Kitten or Little Devil because I'm starting to think there isn't a difference?"

She whimpers behind my hand as I continue. "All this time, I've been watching you. Never once did I think you were in with Lockhart. Nothing ever gets past me, Kaz, nothing, yet here we are. Me, letting my dick get in the way of what's really important and you," I slam her head back again and she cries out in pain. "You, using your pussy like the fucking slut I always knew you were. You played us. Was this your fucking plan?" I grit out. She tries to shake her head no, but there isn't much wiggle room with how I've got her pinned. "Liar. That's what you are. A fucking liar, but don't worry, I've got a special place for you."

I drop my hand from her mouth as I reach into my pocket. "Please," she wheezes out, attempting to catch her breath. "Let me explain."

I squeeze her neck tighter. "Shut the fuck up." When she sees the syringe I've pulled out, she drops both her hands and pushes them up between us to grab my shoulders. In one quick motion, she knees me, preparing to break away. Unfortunately for her, I've already seen it coming and turn just enough for her to miss her mark. I yank her back by her hair and pull her flush against my body before whispering in her ear. "You didn't think you were the only trained fighter did you?" I chuckle as I slide the syringe in her neck and her body goes limp. Jonathan and I train multiple days a week and have since we escaped the hell hole from our childhood. He clearly never told her about that either. I sigh out loud and pull my phone out to make a call.

"Please tell me there's a case I need to be out there for?" Andre asks when he picks up.

"We have a fucking problem," I grit out.

I hear someone scream in the background before a door clicks shut and it goes quiet on his end.

"Fuck sorry," he says, sounding very annoyed. "Is this one of those worst case scenario kind of problems?"

I don't bother beating around the bush. "I'm going to need the vault."

Andre blows out a breath. "Okay, I'll let Antonio know. I'll catch the next flight out."

"Andre," I say, pausing because I'm not really sure what I'm feeling in this moment. "Don't say anything to the guys."

Chapter 27

Kaz

I wake up with an insane headache. My skull literally feels like someone took a chainsaw to it before bashing it with a club. What the fuck happened? I groan and twist my head to the side, but when I try to reach up to rub my temple, my hand won't move. My eyes immediately snap open, only to be met with darkness.

"Nice of you to finally join me, Kitten," I hear Jamison speak smoothly. He sounds robotic, and it's slightly unnerving. I'm hit with sudden flashes of my meeting with the secret texter who turned out to be Lockhart. The memory of Jamison pulling me into the alley hits me next, and I cringe internally.

"Ja...Jamison?" I ask, silently sending out a prayer that this is all just a horrible nightmare. "Where am I? Why can't I move?" I shift my body and try to lift up my arms to make a point. My awareness slowly becomes clearer. I'm on my back, strapped to something flat. Something is wrapped around my face, covering my eyes as well because I can see light peaking through the underneath. All I can think about are all of the times my mom's boyfriend, Pete, had cornered me, smelling of drugs, cigarettes and booze. Making lewd comments and pressing his body against me. My claustrophobia kicks in and I start to hyperventilate. Jamison, wherever he is, doesn't say a word as I lay on the cold surface shaking.

"Jamison, please," I whimper. "Unstrap me. This is insane."

I feel his menacing presence before I hear him. He's so fucking close, I can feel his breathe skating over my face. "Insane would be someone applying for a job at Bolt Corporation with doctored credentials, only to spend fucking years getting close to anyone in upper management. Insane would be sleeping with them to give information to their enemy, knowing it could destroy them. That. Is. Insane!" He's practically screaming in my face now. I've never heard him this unhinged before. Suddenly, I'm glad that I'm blindfolded.

"It's not what you think. I wasn't doing any of those things."

My blindfold is ripped off and I'm left staring into Jamison's eyes. The blue is gone, his eyes so dark, they practically look black. I squint at the bright lights and whip my head around to gauge where I'm at. This place is large and the walls are lined with all kinds of tools. Mechanic shop? Not a chance. More like an operating room. My blood runs cold. Jamison smirks when I look back at him.

"You're a fucking liar. You're a very good fucking liar though, Kaz." he sneers. I hate the way he says my name instead of the nickname he's called me for years. I didn't even like that fucking nickname but now, in this moment, I would be happy if he called me Kitten for the rest of my life. "I'll give you credit. You most definitely pulled one over on me. Now Jonathan, he leads with his heart, so I'm sure he was an easy target. Me though? I'll admit I dropped the ball with you. I won't ever make that mistake again." He walks away from me and I strain my neck to see what he's doing over my shoulder. He comes back into my vision holding a small scalpel.

"Let's start with a few easy questions. How long have you been working for Lockhart?"

That's easy, I think to myself before blurting out, "I haven't!"

He places the scalpel against my dress and drags it completely down, effectively cutting it in half. The cool air hits my body immediately, and I watch as Jamison's eyes light up and he licks his lips. "The Devil really does wear a beautiful disguise."

He presses the scalpel against the skin on my stomach

and drags it just enough to make me bleed. "I haven't Jamison, I swear. I didn't even know it was Lockhart messaging me," I whimper.

He looks at me quizzically, before glaring at me. "Still fucking lying," he says and drags the scalpel further, making me scream out in pain. "Maybe I won't kill you. Maybe I'll drop you off at The Cellar instead, hmm. Would you like that? That's what your boss wanted you to do anyway." He grabs my cheeks, squeezing hard as he gets in my face.

I glare back at him. Of course, he would assume that's what Lockhart had meant. That he wanted me for sex.

"That's not what he was talking about," I grit out from between his fingers. I don't have time to explain because Jamison's phone rings, cutting us both off. He glares back at me before shoving the blindfold in my mouth and holding it in with his hand.

"Hello," he answers with his other hand. He nods his head to himself and after a good thirty seconds replies with a curt, "of course." He hangs up the phone before dropping the scalpel on a tray I hadn't noticed before.

"I have business to attend to. I'll be back, and when I am, you better have your story straight, Kaz. That will make the difference in whether you die quick, or slow and painful."

He leaves me there, half naked, strapped down, the blindfold still shoved in my mouth.

Chapter 28

Jonathan

'Something is off with my brother', I think as I look over at him during our meeting. He looks tense. Not his normal tense either. We have been in this meeting for at least thirty minutes, and he hasn't stopped fidgeting since. Jamison never fidgets.

"You okay?" I whisper when Xavier and Sebastian start discussing some case they are both dealing with.

"Yes," he states, matter of factly.

My brows scrunch up. Asking my brother if he's okay is usually foreign to me. Normally it's the other way around. Normally I'm the one needing consoling. He doesn't elaborate.

"Have you heard from Kaz?" I ask him, trying to change the subject when I realize he isn't going to continue the conversation. His head whips towards me quickly and I see a brief flicker of emotion cross his face before he schools himself. Well, that's interesting.

"No, I haven't, why?" he asks me, his voice wavering the slightest bit.

He's lying. Call it twin intuition or a sixth sense. Call it whatever the fuck you want but if there's one thing I know for certain, it's that he's lying right now.

"I haven't heard from her all day. As a matter of fact, I haven't heard from her since yesterday. Apparently she texted Sebastian she was sick, but she's not responding to my messages." I say, looking Jamison directly in the eyes. He doesn't say a word.

"She hasn't texted you at all? I just think it's weird she wouldn't at least respond to me, ya know?"

Jamison continues to stare at me before looking down at his phone and then up at me again. "No, no contact at all."

Something is going on with him, but he's clearly not going to give in, so I choose to drop the conversation for now. Fifteen minutes later, we are leaving our meeting when Jamison's phone beeps. I peer over at him to see he's whipped his phone out and is staring intently at the screen. As soon as he notices I'm staring, he shoves his phone back into his pocket.

"I have to go," he mutters before turning and walking away.

There's a slight pause before my mind starts reeling, and I know with one hundred percent certainty that I need to follow my brother. Unfortunately, it's like the universe has another plan, because Sebastian stops me from out of nowhere.

"We need to discuss a few things, Jonathan."

"Can they wait?" I ask, looking over his shoulder. "I'm kind of in a hurry."

Sebastian peers over his shoulder, but Jamison is already out of sight. He looks back at me before sighing. "Listen, I'm not fucking stupid. Whatever you and Jamison have going on with Kaz needs to be discussed."

That stops me in my tracks and I immediately zero in on his face. He doesn't look angry. In fact, he looks worried. Sebastian never looks worried.

"Uh..." I start, looking down at my shoes, but he cuts me off.

"I know I said she was off limits, but I also know something has been going on for years. Either way, we need to all sit down and figure out how this could play out. There's too many parties involved and I can't risk you and your brother having issues with each other over a woman."

My head snaps back up to him and I grin, making him frown. "You think she's going to cause a rift between us?" I ask, laughing. "I don't mind her getting in between us, Sebastian, but not in the way you're thinking."

"Jonathan," he growls out. "I'm fucking serious."

"I know, I know," I reply, backing around him with my hands up. "I really have to go, but I swear, we will continue this conversation later," I say as I walk backwards. He huffs out as he turns and stalks away. I make my break for it and shoot down the elevator. Annoyance flickers when I don't see my brother's car in the parking garage, so I pull my phone out and click the tracking app he had installed. I never use this shit but desperate times and all that.

"Shit," I curse under my breath as I pocket my phone and start my bike up. He's about ten minutes out and still on the move. If I drive fast, I might be able to catch up to him, wherever he's going. I feel tense, but it's not my own emotions. My brother's turmoil swirls inside my brain, wrecking me down to my soul. Whatever the fuck he's going to do right now, it can't be good. He might not recover from this.

Twenty minutes later, I'm pulling up to the vault. I stare at the large building, perplexed. Why would he be here without telling the rest of us? I make my way over to the door and enter the code, hearing the lock click open. The door opens quietly, but I'm not prepared for what I see when I walk in. Jamison hovers over Kaz's body, gliding a very sharp scalpel up one of her legs. Her blood trickles down her thigh, pooling on the table she's currently tied to. Her eyes are scrunched tightly closed, but I can see the tears trickling down her face as she cries out into the gag.

"What the fuck are you doing?" I bellow out in rage. Jamison whips around, a scowl on his face. My fist connects with his nose and his head snaps back. His eyes widen in surprise as he wipes under his nose, revealing blood on the back of his hand.

"I'm taking care of the problem," he grits out, looking back towards Kaz. "She's been playing with us all along."

"You have had it out for her this whole time!" I yell out. "At this point, I feel like you want something to be wrong." He stares at me, his gaze hard. "When do we just get to be happy, brother?" I sigh. His eyes soften a bit and I can see he's conflicted, but he doesn't get a chance to react as a blur of motion behind him causes both our gazes to swing behind him. Kaz jumps down from the table, the scalpel in her hand held up high. Jamison must have dropped it when I walked in.

"Here Kitten, Kitten," my brother taunts as he rushes Kaz, attempting to grab her. That earns him a swift kick to the ribs when she delivers the most beautiful roundhouse I've ever seen. Where the fuck did that come from? My brother doubles over and she makes her break towards the door. I grab her arm, hauling her back towards me and feel the sting of her blade when the scalpel cuts right down my cheek.

Chapter 29

Kaz

The scalpel slips from my fingers as Jonathan swipes his cheek, looking at the blood that coats his fingers, before back at me.

"You cut me, Pretty Girl," he states with wide eyes.

"I'm, I'm sorry. I'm so sorry," I reply as I try to pull from his grip. Jamison's already up and moving towards us with clear intention written all over his face.

"I didn't do what he said. I fucking swear it. I didn't know it was Lockhart messaging me. You have to believe me," I plead out.

"Bullshit," Jamison seethes out. He picks the scalpel up from the ground and pushes me up against the wall. My gut reaction is to struggle, so that's exactly what I do. My hands immediately go up to his hand to rip it off of me, but Jonathan is faster. He pushes Jamison back a step, coming in between us. "Let her fucking speak."

Jamison stands up straight, glaring at his brother. "I don't need to hear any more fucking lies from her."

He's not going to believe anything I fucking say at this point. I already know it. He has his mind made up, and I need solid proof. I need a minute to think about this. I can't fight or argue my way out of this one, at least not with Jamison. He doesn't operate that way. And then it hits me. I know what he needs. The only thing that will stop him long enough for me to convince them I'm innocent. The one thing so fucking hard for me to give. Submission. Jamison and Jonathan are still arguing as I drop to my knees and bow my head. The floor is cold and hard and I'm forced to bite my lip to stop myself from voicing out my irritation. Silence envelopes me when they both realize what I've done.

"Pretty Girl?" Jonathan questions.

"What the fuck are you doing, Kaz? Jamison asks.

I look up at him and meet his glare. He's so fucking angry, he looks possessed. I've never seen him look at me this way, not even when I thought he hated me all these years. "Please," I plead out. "Give me a chance to prove it to you. If you still don't believe me after that, then kill me." And I mean it. I really fucking do because if I don't have this anymore, this life I've created with not only my career, but both of these men, then I don't have anything worth living for.

"Start talking," Jamison grits out. And I do. I tell them about the cab driver and what he said. I tell them about the messages I received afterwards from the unknown number. I tell them about swiping Jamison's toothbrush for the anonymous person who texted me. The last part makes them both scrunch their brows. I feel like I have so much more to say, but suddenly, I'm so fucking tired. The little energy I had left from being held hostage by Jamison has dissipated and before I know it, my eyes are closing and I'm fading into the darkness.

I wake to the feeling of warmth surrounding me. Warm water and a warm body holding me from behind. I'm too tired to open my eyes at first, so I sit and relish in the fact that someone is washing me. I feel the washcloth as it glides down my arm before it goes back up and proceeds to do the same thing to the other. The smell of lavender surrounds me and the sounds of running water and soft music soothe me. Am I dead or am I dreaming? The washcloth dips down into the water, just barely grazing my breast. My nipple immediately hardens and I moan out in response, causing the washcloth to stop in its tracks.

"You awake, Pretty Girl?" Jonathan's voice rasps out. My eyes immediately snap open to find myself in Jonathan's bathroom. In Jonathan's sunken tub, with him enveloping me from behind. It's only then that I become aware of his hardened length pressing up against my lower back. I tense up, gripping both of his thighs tightly when the memories of him, his brother and I at the vault come rushing back.

"Easy baby," he says, running his hands down my arms to soothe me. "You're safe. You're always safe with me."

"Where's your brother?" I ask as I turn towards the bathroom door. I'm fully expecting him to break in and drown me in this tub. I can't help it as the paranoia creeps in.

Jonathan twists me just a little so that I'm sitting in his lap sideways and grabs my chin to turn my face towards him. "Jamison isn't here right now. He's out. He's figuring out some things. There's so many things we don't really understand right now."

"Is he...does he believe me now?" I ask him, peering up into his eyes. They are such a bright shade of blue, I almost feel like I'm looking into the sky when I'm looking at him. My eyes trail to his cheek where I see the gash I cut into him. My fingers reach up to touch it, causing him to hiss in pain and grab my wrist. "I'm so sorry, Jonathan," I whisper.

"It's okay," he replies, dragging my hand down and placing it on his chest instead. "You were scared you were going to lose everything. Jamison told me all about your past. I understand."

My fingers trail across his chest and down his perfect abs. He knows. He knows I'm a fraud. He knows I've been living in this half truth for years and he's still here. He's still fucking here, washing me in his tub. Taking care of me. I swing my legs around to straddle him, causing the warm water to slosh over the side of the tub. I just need to be close to him. I want to be close to someone who knows the real me and doesn't give a damn. He sucks in a sharp breath when I lean into him, causing me to hesitate. I can feel the length of him pressed up against my pussy. The thought of him being inside me immediately sends flutters to the pit of my stomach. He must still want me, right?

"Fuck," he groans out when my hips grind just the

slightest against him. "Are you sure?"

"Touch me, Jonathan," I plead, grinding against him again and throwing my head back. He grips my ass with both hands and pulls me closer before licking and kissing up my shoulder and neck. He rolls me against his dick, gliding me back and forth, sending little zaps out every time he hits my clit. Before I know what's happening, my orgasm comes barreling out of me full force. I cry out as he continues to rub himself between my folds.

"Need to be inside you, Pretty Girl." he grits out as he grabs my face with one hand and devours my lips. "Tell me it's okay to fuck you, baby."

"Yes," I cry out, lifting my hips.

He lets go of my face and grabs my ass again, this time lifting and positioning me above his very hard dick. In one swift motion, he glides me down onto him and continues to devour my mouth, swallowing my moans. He uses the water to his full advantage, gliding me up and down while fucking me from underneath. I can already feel another orgasm threatening to unravel itself as his pounds into me.

"I fucking love you, Pretty Girl," Jonathan states, before dragging me into another kiss. He moves inside me, picking up his pace, not giving me any time to process his words. "I love you," he says, as he peppers kisses along my neck and brings his hand between us to rub against my clit. "I don't care where you come from."

My orgasm builds like a volcano ready to erupt.

"I've loved you from the minute I saw you. I don't care who you were before we met. All that matters is who you are to me now, and it's everything. You are everything to me, Kaz," he whispers while moving faster inside me. His words send me over the edge. I'm free falling and he's right behind me. We both come together, our moans ringing out around us as we kiss passionately. When I pull away and look at him, I'm prepared to see remorse or regret for saying those things in the heat of the moment. I'm shocked to see him smiling. A genuinely happy smile as he pushes a lock of hair out of my face and behind my ear.

"You love me?" I ask him, still waiting for the other shoe to drop.

"I do," he replies. "And I don't expect you to res…" I silence him with my finger over his lips.

"I love you too," I reply before pulling my finger away and kissing him again. He groans into my mouth and I feel him already hardening inside me again.

"You're insatiable," I whisper before lifting my hips up and dropping them again.

He grips my hips, helping lift me to repeat the motion and I feel him grin against my mouth before replying, "When it comes to you, Pretty Girl. You have no idea."

Chapter 30

Jamison

"Jonathan has her at our place," I state as I stand against Xavier's kitchen island, staring at both him and Sebastian.

Xavier looks flustered. "Why didn't you tell us what was going on?"

I look at him with a straight face. "I didn't think it was necessary. Andre was aware there was a situation. That's as far as I thought it needed to go."

"Not good enough," Sebastian growls out. "Dammit, Jamison. This could have blown up in our faces. You could have fucking killed her!"

Both Riley and Corrine choose to walk into the kitchen at that exact moment. The laughter dies out and smiles drop from both their faces.

"What's going on?" Riley asks Sebastian.

Corrine turns to Xavier. "Could have killed who?"

Both men turn to me expectantly. I groan internally, trying to decide how to backtrack out of this conversation.

"Shouldn't you two be watching some chick flick right now in the bedroom? This was supposed to be a private conversation."

"We were hungry," Corrine says with her hands on her hips. "Don't change the subject."

Suddenly, Riley's head whips towards me again, and her eyes narrow. "Did you find Kaz, Jamison?"

"That's what we were discussing, Little Mouse," Sebastian says, pulling Riley's hair over her shoulder and kissing her neck. I roll my eyes at how pathetic he has become these days, and then I remember how badly I've wanted to do that exact thing to Kaz many times before.

"Is this about Kaz?" Riley yells out, attempting to walk around the island to me. Thankfully, Sebastian grabs her, hauling her back to him and yanking her onto his lap."

"Kaz is fine. Calm down," he says in her ear.

Xavier isn't quick enough though because Corrine is in my face when I turn towards her. "What did you do to her, Jamison?" She shrieks and pushes me backwards. I grab both of her wrists, causing Xavier to jump up with wide eyes and grab her before I can react further. I let go of her quickly and hold my hands up when I see the look of fear on his face. He knows me too well. He knows I don't like to be pushed around and he knows how I would normally react in this situation. For once, though, I'm not even angry. I deserved that. I deserve much more than that after the information I've scraped together. Part of me thinks I was trying so hard to find something wrong with Kaz that I ignored some of the things I would usually find so easily. For instance, I could have looked up Kaz's text history between her and Lockhart. Hell, I've invaded her privacy like that many times before. One look would have told me everything I needed to know. That Kaz, indeed, did not know who was messaging her. That she was certainly being blackmailed and that she definitely did not want to do what he was asking of her. Am I angry she stole my fucking toothbrush? Fuck yes I am, but I also believe she thought she had no choice in the matter. It's not like I gave her much of a choice either over the years. I've kept her secret and held it over her head. I've used her and her secrets to my advantage. I won't say I regret that because it would be a lie. I loved every moment it gave me with her but do I know I'll have to pay for that at some point. Yes, yes I do.

"I wasn't going to do anything, Xavier," I say, with my hands still up. He looks at me and nods as he pulls Corrine closer to him. She looks at him perplexed, probably wondering why he was so worried. She should be thanking him. If she was any other stranger outside of our circle, I would have snapped both of her wrists without a second thought.

"Kaz isn't who you think she is," I say. It's time to rip off the bandaid. "She's been lying from the very beginning. She lied about what school she went to. She lied about graduating. She lied about where she came from. The biggest lie was her pretending she was weak and fragile when really she could probably hold her own, one on one, against most men larger than her."

"Wait what?" Xavier asks.

"She learned how to hack and fight from a friend when she was younger. Her hacking skills were adequate at most, enough to get past all of you, I guess. The fighting though. She can hold her own," I say, smirking to myself as I remember her kick to my ribs. She left a beautiful bruise, she will never see because of the ink that covers my body.

"Are you saying you knew about her resume?" Sebastian grits out, clearly annoyed. "Why the fuck would you have let this go on?"

I sigh before continuing with what I know will irritate him further. "One, I didn't see her as a liability and two, both my brother and I have been fucking around with her this entire time."

"Unbelievable," Sebastian growls just as both Riley and Corrine look at each other and exclaim "I knew it!"

Xavier doesn't say a word.

"I knew something was going on, but I didn't know how far back this really went. You understand the position this puts all of us in, right? What am I supposed to do now, Jamison. What happens when you both decide you're done fucking around with her and she gets angry? What happens if you both want something serious with her and she has to choose? You have to fucking see the problem we have here." Sebastian stares at me expectantly, waiting for a response.

"Right now, I'm sure the last person she wants is me, Sebastian. It won't cause an issue at work, that I can promise."

"We can't get rid of her," Xavier states out of nowhere.

"She's literally the best we have ever had in Human Resources. Besides, who gives a fuck if her credentials are fake. No one outside of our circle needs to know that."

Sebastian nods his head in agreement, bringing a smile to Riley's face. "He's right. She is the best we have had. Firing her would do the company more harm than good. We can all agree on that. This Lockhart thing, though. How the fuck did Kaz get involved with him?"

I hold my finger up to stop him as I dial Andre's phone and he answers the facetime call. I've already discussed a little bit with him, but not everything. I quickly catch him up before continuing.

"That's just it. I did quite a bit of digging. I don't think Kaz even realized how close she was to that circle. Like I said before, she fought in the underground when she was younger. It's how she survived, seeing as how her mom is a junkie and her dad was never in the picture. It didn't click for me until I read through some of her shit. Little Devil. That was her nickname and guess who gave it to her?"

"Fucking Diablo Degerson," Andre says putting two and two together.

Xavier whistles, "Holy shit. As in Frederick Degerson's uncle?"

"The one and only," Sebastian replies before turning to me. "Are you thinking what I'm thinking right now?"

"If it's that Kaz is possibly the daughter to one of the men in charge of the underground, then yes brother, I am. And if that's the case, this is much bigger than The Triad or The Cellar."

"I don't understand what's going on?" Riley voices with concern.

"Ever heard of the four horsemen, Riley?" Andre cuts in. "Imagine four very prestigious families. Now imagine those families controlling the entire underground. Each family is in charge of one part."

She looks at Sebastian. "Why didn't you tell me all of this when we were meeting with Frederick?"

Sebastian laughs, "Frederick was the least of my concerns. As far as any of us were concerned, he's just a lapdog for his uncle. A playboy and the running joke to his family name. But it does make sense now why he is going after Lockhart. If he can dismember the Triad, he essentially will be taking out a part of one of the Four's businesses."

"Bolt Corporation cannot be involved in any of this," Xavier huffs. "We are a fucking law firm and half these guys are clients."

"That brings me to our final problem," I sigh out when everyone looks at me. "The reason Lockhart was meeting with Kaz. He wanted her to bring him something of mine...She brought him my toothbrush."

The room goes silent. No one says a word as I look at all of them. Background noise from Andre's facetime video causes us all to look at his screen. We catch a quick glimpse of bleach blonde hair before his phone topples over and I hear him cursing in Italian. The call ends and the room is left silent again.

"I'm texting Sasha right now to make sure everything is okay," Xavier says as he types out on his phone.

"Jamison, do you know for sure?" Sebastian asks.

I shake my head no at him. "I need proof and that requires bait," I say, eyeing him for his response.

"Might be our only option," he replies, eyeing me back.

Riley looks at both of us confused. "I don't know what you both have planned but Corrine and I want to see Kaz. Take us there now, please." She stands up, immediately grabbing her purse and Corrine does the same.

Chapter 31

Kaz

    I'm sitting on the couch in Jonathan's living room, him next to me, when Jamison walks in. My whole body tenses up when we lock eyes. What is he thinking right now? Is he even sorry? The look on his face is completely blank which pisses me the fuck off. How dare he come in here and act like he didn't just torture me over nothing. Jonathan leans in front of me, breaking my eye contact with his brother.

    "You okay, Pretty Girl?"

    I nod yes at him before looking over his shoulder to find Riley and Corrine walking into the apartment. I jump up, a smile immediately forming on my face. They both run over and hug me.

    "Are you okay, Kaz?" Riley asks concerned.

    Corrine looks at Jamison with narrowed eyes. "We heard what happened."

    "It was just a slight miscommunication," I try to reason, knowing full well I have a shit ton of secrets I'm still keeping from them.

    "Bullshit," Corrine seethes out, still eyeing Jamison.

    Xavier comes up behind her and wraps his arms around her before whispering in her ear. Her shoulders slump a little and her eyes soften. "We are really glad you're okay, Kaz."

    Fuck, I feel so bad right now. These girls have been so good to me and I've kept so much shit from them. From everyone, really. I'm so tired. I'm tired of trying to keep everything straight. I'm tired of trying to keep track of every little lie. I look back at Jonathan. He's been too fucking good to me and now he knows everything. He still loves me after all I've put him through. Maybe I just need to come clean with everyone. Maybe if I let everything out now, there's still a chance I can salvage these relationships. I might not have a job at Bolt Corporation, but I can find some other way to make ends meet. I've saved enough money over the years to get me by until I figure something else out.

"I have to tell you all some things. I've kept a lot of secrets and I think it's best I just lay it all out there." I say with a steady voice.

"Unnecessary," Sebastian responds coolly. "Jamison already informed us of everything."

My head whips to Jamison and I glare at him. "He told you everything, did he?" I reply to Sebastian. Jamison's gaze doesn't waver.

"Yes, Kaz," Xavier responds. "He told us about your resume and schooling. He also told us about some other family dynamics as well and unless you have a bigger secret than being a fucking ninja, I think it's all covered."

"How nice of you to finally decide when it was appropriate for you to spill my secrets," I seethe out as I stalk over to Jamison. He leans against the wall with his hands in his pockets like he doesn't have any care in the world. "Were you just waiting for the perfect time to upend my entire life?"

Jamison stares at me but doesn't say a word. No one does.

"Answer me," I scream. The sound of my palm cracking against his cheek echoes throughout the apartment. His face whips to the side before he turns slowly back towards me. His lip is bleeding and his eyes are the deepest shade of blue. So dark, that if I didn't know any better, I would think they were black. Jonathan grabs me around my waist from behind in an attempt to pull me away, but Jamison is too quick. His hand snatches my wrist pulling both me and Jonathan towards him. My body is yanked flush against his with Jonathan sandwiching me between them.

"Jamison, don't," Jonathan hisses as my chin is gripped

tight and I'm forced to look up into the dark abyss swirling in Jamison's eyes.

He leans into my face, close enough for only Jonathan and I to hear him. "I deserved that, Kitten, but it will only happen once. The next time you place your hands on me, it will be because I'm fucking you within an inch of your life."

I'm stunned silent. I have literally zero brain function in this moment. All I can think of is the warmth at my core and the wetness between my thighs. How can someone I despise make me feel like this? Jamison lets go of my chin as Jonathan pulls me away. I turn towards the others to find Sebastian and Xavier holding tightly to both Riley and Corrine. Riley's expression is worried, while Corrine looks downright angry.

"Before this gets out of hand," Sebastian states, breaking the tense silence. "Kaz, we have all collectively agreed to not fire you."

"Wait, what?" I ask, confused.

"Well, yeah. Umm, we were getting to that part. You've worked for us for so long and let's face it, no one can do as good a job as you. With or without a perfect resume."

"You guys are serious?" I ask, looking between them both as they nod yes. "All of you?" I ask, looking at Jamison. He nods his head and for a brief moment, I see a flicker of some kind of emotion flash in his eyes. "Thank you," I murmur out, trying not to read too much into it.

"There's another thing we need to discuss," Sebastian says, eyeing me. "I put a call into Frederick Degerson on my way over here. We have a meeting set up with his uncle tomorrow at Bolt Corporation. I think this is something you are going to need to be there for."

He proceeds to tell me all about the information they've uncovered. I don't know what they expect me to do or how they expect me to react, but dread pools in the pit of my stomach. Diablo could be my father, and if that's the case, he could very well be the reason for Ben's disappearance.

Chapter 32

Jonathan

I'm sitting in our meeting room with Kaz to my left. Jamison sits on her other side. Sebastian and Xavier sit at the head of the table to my right. Corrine is with Riley in her office while she goes over some paperwork. Andre's face peers at all of us through the large screen video call. He looks tired as fuck with bags under his eyes. I've never seen him this disheveled.

"Are you sure you have it all covered down there? I'm worried." Xavier says to him.

I look at both of them. "What's going on?"

Andre straightens his suit jacket, sitting up straight. "Apparently someone on my property has been sneaking inside and messing with…things…" He trails off, lost in thought.

"Things?" I question, urging him to continue.

He seems to snap out of it before replying and shaking his head. "Uh, yeah. Just random stuff going on over here. I've installed more surveillance and am certain we will catch whoever it is soon enough. Probably one of the younger staff members we have recently hired." He looks over at Xavier through the screen. "Either way, it will be taken care of. Sasha is perfectly safe here."

Xavier looks like he wants to continue the conversation, but we are interrupted by a knock on the door. An assistant swings the door open when Sebastian calls out to them and in walks Diablo Degerson. He walks in wearing a tailored black Armani suit, his light blonde hair styled back perfectly. Specks of grey pepper throughout it as he turns his gaze, his green eyes zeroing in on Kaz. She grabs my hand immediately under the table and I feel her squeeze tightly. My response is to slide my chair closer to her. Apparently, Jamison has the same idea. Diablo eyes us both with interest.

"May I?" He asks Sebastian, gesturing to the chair directly across from Kaz.

Sebastian nods and replies, "Of course."

"Hello, Little Devil," Diablo says with a smile. "It's been a very long time."

Kaz doesn't respond right away, making Diablo's eyebrows scrunch up in confusion. He looks around at all of us for guidance, but we are just as confused as him. I squeeze her hand, hoping it gives her some sort of support.

"I'm not fighting anymore," she blurts out suddenly. "I hope you didn't come here to try to bring me back."

"Of course not," he growls out. "I didn't want you there in the first place. Had I known who you were to me in the beginning, I never would have allowed it."

"So it's true?" Sebastian asks."She's your daughter?"

"Of course she's mine," he states plainly.

Kaz looks at him with wide eyes. "Why didn't you tell me?"

"Well, for starters, I didn't know for certain until right before you left. Your junkie mother came to me on one of her binges, threatening to tell my wife about you. Apparently she found some money hidden in your room and it was banded with my logo. Your winnings, I'm assuming. It must have jogged her memory."

Kaz holds up her hand to quiet him. "Wait. You and my mother?"

He grimaces, clearly uncomfortable with the conversation. "Once, before I was married. She was working at one of the clubs. I was heavily intoxicated, among other things"

"Stop," Kaz says. "I don't need details. I'm very aware of my mother's escapades."

His eyes soften a bit. "Had I known about you, I never

would have allowed you to grow up in that environment."

"Oh, bullshit," I interrupt. "Your family is involved in the underground. Who knows what kind of danger she would have been in."

He turns to me and glares. "Watch your mouth. No daughter of mine would have ever been in any danger. I have certain protections in place."

"I know exactly what happens in places connected to the underground," I grit out as I lean over the table. "I know…"

"Enough," Jamison says loudly, cutting me off. I turn towards him with a glare. He nods at Kaz, who is looking down into her lap.

"Fuck, I'm sorry, Pretty Girl," I say, grabbing her hand again. She squeezes mine back.

"I want to know what happened to Ben," she says to Diablo, sitting up straighter in her chair.

I look around to see everyone except my brother and Diablo, just as confused as I am. I feel a slight twinge of jealousy. Who the fuck is Ben?

"What happened to him? He went missing and no one can find him? Did you have something to do with it?"

It hits me then, who she is talking about. The friend from her childhood that she has pictured on her phone screen.

"I had nothing to do with his disappearance, Kaz, I promise. I was monitoring his contact with you and one day he vanished. I tried looking more into it, but no one would talk. He had to have pissed off someone else in The Four."

"You knew where I was? Why didn't you come after me?" She eyes him skeptically.

He sighs. "As I said, I didn't want you involved in the underground anymore. You were safe where you were and you were doing well for yourself. I had an account set up for you in the event you ever needed anything. I didn't want to upend your life. Now I see that was a mistake. You ended up a part of my world anyway," he says, eyeing the rest of us. "Regardless, the money is yours and I've already placed it in your name. Use it or not. It's up to you."

Kaz chooses to ignore that statement and instead asks another question. "Does your wife know about me?"

The question catches us all off guard except Diablo, who smiles before answering. "She does now and she would love to meet you. You also have a younger brother, although he might be harder to get ahold of. He's in college and…temperamental."

Kaz smiles and I can tell it's genuine. "I can't wait."

"There's the matter of Frederick," Sebastian cuts in.

"Ahh, yes, my nephew. Unfortunately, I cannot get involved in that matter. However, I can assure you that Kaz will remain safe." He looks down at his watch before standing quickly. "I have another matter to attend to, but I am free to discuss some possible business opportunities another time?"

Sebastian nods his head at Diablo, who then turns to Kaz. "I will message you with details soon. I really am so glad to finally be able to have you in my life again."

He turns to me and then to my brother. "In the meantime, she will be kept safely out of harm's way, correct?"

I glare at him before muttering, "of course." Jamison merely nods.

Chapter 33

Jamison

'This prick has some nerve addressing Jonathan and I about Kaz's safety,' I think, as I watch him walk out of the office.

"Well that didn't really get us anywhere, did it? I mean, I have more questions than I did to begin with," Xavier says to no one in particular. "We still have zero information on Frederick and why the fuck he would be going after Lockhart on the sly."

Andre huffs out in annoyance. "I'll see if I can find out any information from my father. I'm supposed to be meeting him tonight anyway."

Sebastian nods his head to Andre before the screen goes blank. "So, I think we should probably discuss the Lockhart situation." He places his hands together and rests his chin on them before looking directly at Kaz. "He wanted Jamison's toothbrush, correct?"

"Yes," Kaz says before looking at me guilty. "He asked for that or his brush with hair in it but when I looked at his brush, there wasn't even one strand of hair, so I opted for the toothbrush. I'm well aware he was obviously wanting DNA, but you guys are adopted so I didn't think it would really matter." She looks down at her lap as she says the last sentence.

I turn to Jonathan, who nods his head at me. We have already discussed what we suspected after my incident with Kaz at The Vault. Now seems like the best time to rip off the bandaid. "Jonathan and I both think we are Lockhart's sons. We obviously aren't one hundred percent certain, but it seems like a very high possibility. The only question we have is why Lockhart would need my DNA if he already had that paper Sasha saw, stating he had a child."

"Holy shit, that would make so much sense," Xavier says, rubbing his chin. "Of course he wouldn't be worried about me, or Sasha for that matter. We signed our rights to his kingdom over, but you didn't, and if that's the case, you guys would have been first in line all along."

Jonathan shakes his head angrily. "We don't want any part of that place. If it burned to the ground tomorrow, I would throw a fucking party and piss on it's ashes."

"I have to agree with Jonathan. We would gladly sign over our rights. I also wouldn't mind starting another fire there seeing as how my last attempt only burned down a small portion," I say smirking at Xavier. He laughs out loud, no doubt remembering our last incident at The Cellar.

"The issue is, we haven't seen Lockhart out and about at all recently. I think he is being a bit more careful but we need something to lure him out. In fact, the last time he came out was to meet with Kaz," Sebastian says. He looks at me and we both turn to look at Kaz. She looks at both of us before her eyes go wide, the realization of what we are implying finally hitting her.

"Absolutely fucking not," Jonathan yells, as he stands up from his chair and slams his hands on the table in front of him. "We aren't using her as bait. Are you both out of your fucking minds?"

I sigh out loud. "We wouldn't be leaving her alone, Jonathan. Besides, I'm pretty sure she can handle her own against Lockhart if it comes down to it."

"No," Jonathan practically growls before grabbing Kaz's hand and pulling her from seat. "Come on, Pretty Girl. Let's go get some food and curl up on the couch for a movie."

Kaz looks over at me, biting her lip. She looks torn, but the motion of her grazing her teeth against her plump bottom lip, sends blood rushing right down to my dick. Fuck, this woman is going to be the death of me.

"Jonathan," I say, gritting my teeth. It's taking everything in me not to show my frustration right now, which is unusual.

Normally, it's much easier to feign nonchalance. The way he is dragging Kaz away from me like a caveman is bringing me closer to the edge than I want to be right now. I follow behind as he whispers whatever shit he's saying to her. Both Xavier and Sebastian are right behind me.

"I think we need to discuss this," Sebastian says, as we all enter the elevator.

Jonathan pulls Kaz against his chest, embracing her from behind. "Discuss possibly putting Kaz in danger?"

Xavier cuts in before Sebastian can snap back. "Come on, Jonathan, you know we wouldn't put her in danger." The elevator doors open and we all walk out into the main lobby on the ground floor. Xavier walks backwards in front of us while continuing to plead his case. "This could get us the information we need. Don't you want to know? She wouldn't be left alone."

"She's not fucking doing it," Jonathan says, gripping her arms tightly with both hands.

"She is right fucking here, brother," I practically scream in Jonathan's face. My patience has finally snapped and I can see Kaz cringe back the smallest amount at my explosion. Jonathan doesn't respond, clearly surprised at my outburst. "She's right here, dammit," I say again, a little calmer. "And she's a big girl. Kaz can make her own decisions, can't you, Kitten?"

A raucous ensues behind me by the front lobby doors and we all turn around to see what is causing chaos. Holy fucking shit. What impeccable timing this man has. The two doormen we have catch the half naked man by his arms just as he drops to his knees not ten feet from me. He's dirty as fuck, shoeless and wearing the same small briefs he was in the last time I saw him. His collar is still attached, the metal chain dragging against the floor, as my men proceed to haul him back up to his feet.

"Stop," I say, as my eyes meet his and I see the recognition come over him. My men drop both of his arms and he makes it a few more feet closer to me before crashing back down on his hands and knees. "Bolt Corporation," he wheezes out. "You said to find Bolt Corporation."

"Indeed," I murmur, just as Kaz pushes around me to see what is happening. Her eyes go round as saucers when she sees the man on the floor. "Be...Ben?"

"Kaz?" He questions.

"Oh my god, Ben!" She rushes him, dropping to her knees and wrapping her arms around him tightly. He hugs her back before they both break down, sobbing.

I feel Jonathan come up quickly to my right and put my arm up to stop him from going further.

"Who the fuck is that? Why is he naked? And why the fuck are his arms around our girl?" He states, jealousy written all over his features.

"It's the missing friend." I look at my brother and watch his shoulders relax. "He was in The Cellar."

"You helped him escape?"

I look back to see them still locked in an embrace. "I may have given him my keycard, the last time we were there. The escaping part he did all on his own, though."

"That's what took you so long?" Xavier asks out of nowhere. "You had to go back through the rooms the normal way because you didn't have your keycard anymore."

I watch as the paramedics come in and help Ben onto the gurney.

"Maybe," I say, shrugging my shoulders.

Sebastian looks from Kaz and Ben over to me. "You put yourself in danger for someone you didn't even know."

"He knows Kaz."

All three of them stare at me with eyebrows raised.

"Don't fucking say it," I growl out in warning. I'm in no mood for these pricks to psychoanalyze me right now. The truth is, I have no idea why I helped the man. At that moment, it seemed logical, but now, I'm questioning myself.

"What's going on?" I hear Riley ask Sebastian as she steps up with Corrine and my intern, Kyle.

Kyle looks over towards the gurney with a small smile. "Yeah, and who is the sexy, half naked God that stumbled into our firm?"

"Wipe the drool from your chin, Kyle," Xavier says, laughing. "It's Kaz's childhood friend who went missing years ago.

"Dammit, the sexy ones are always straight. Do you think they're childhood sweethearts?" Kyle questions, while watching the scene before him.

"No," Jonathan and I both growl out in unison, making him smirk at both of us.

We follow them out to the ambulance and watch as they load Ben into the back. Kaz jumps in next to him, still holding his hand. She looks over at all of us, her eyes still wet from crying. "I'll do it."

No one says a word as both doors slam shut and we watch the ambulance drive away. Jonathan already has his helmet strapped on and he's walking towards his bike. "I'll follow them to make sure they're safe."

"Good," Sebastian yells at Jonathan as he starts his bike. "And quit fucking parking on the damn sidewalk."

"Let's discuss a plan," I say as I watch the ambulance and my brother disappear around the corner. "It's time to take Lockhart down a peg or two."

Chapter 34

Lockhart

There's no faking the paperwork this time. I hand delivered the DNA evidence myself. I look over the results matching Jamison's DNA to mine. How did I not see it? In my defense, I never thought the original paperwork sent to me was real, let alone that it was possibly a match to a twin. How the hell did she get the original DNA to begin with? No matter. All my questions should be answered soon enough.

The door to my office swings open, making me growl out loud.

"I told you to knock," I say without looking up.

"Sorry, sir," one of my newer men says, as he yanks a woman in by her arm. "This one has given me a lot of trouble."

I look up to see her struggling with him as he decides to shove her to the ground.

"That will be all," I reply to him, thoroughly unimpressed. "I cannot fucking wait for Devin to come back. The rest of my men are complete imbeciles. The woman with mousy brown hair looks up at me, her vibrant blue eyes full of hatred.

"Hello, Eve," I say with a smirk. She glares at me from the floor as I stand from my desk and make my way around to her. I squat down in front of her, eyeing her body. She's still as beautiful as I remember, though maybe a bit more frail looking. She could definitely use a few extra meals.

"Did you think I wouldn't be able to find out who sent me that paperwork?"

"I don't know what you're talking about," she says, looking down at the floor. I push a lock of hair behind her ear, causing her body to tense.

"Oh, Eve. I traced that DNA paperwork right back to your shitty little apartment," I reply, with a smile, causing her head to snap back up.

"What DNA paperwork?" She asks me quizzically.

She's fucking good. She genuinely looks like she has no idea what I'm talking about. If I had more time, I would love to play. The truth is, I'm not only out of time, but my patience is running low as well. My hand shoots out and my fingers wrap around her delicate throat.

"No more games," I say, tightening my grip. "You sent me DNA paperwork that matched one of the twins with me. I had my own tests run and they matched up."

Her eyes go wide and she leans away from me. "I didn't send you those papers, Ethan. You were never supposed to find out about them."

"Bullshit!" I scream, slamming her back to the ground as she tries to crawl away from me. "Where the fuck have you been all of this time, huh? Where have you been hiding?" I straddle her as she struggles against my hand still locked around her throat. She purses her lips in defiance, which only serves to piss me off further. I stand up quickly and drag her towards my desk by her hair.

"If you won't answer me, I might as well get some other use from you," I say as I yank her frail body from the ground and bend her over my desk. She's still in the nightgown she wore to bed when my men grabbed her. Leaning over her, I whisper in her ear, "Are you still innocent or did my Vixen learn a thing or two over the years?"

"No, please don't," she cries out. My free hand pushes up under her gown to rip her panties off while my other hand smashes her head to the desk, holding her in place. "Last chance," I say, spitting on my already hard dick and lining it up with her entrance. "Where have you been, Vixen, and why was I unable to find you?"

"I was sent away!" She screams out, making me pause.

"My parents made a deal with yours. Give up the babies and disappear. They paid for everything. They didn't even ask me what I wanted."

"They didn't even give me a choice," she says, sobbing. I rip her head sideways and watch entranced as tears fall down her cheek. The site only makes my dick harder. I lean in and lick her cheek, the salty taste sliding over my tongue.

"Would you have stayed?" I ask her. She eyes me, but doesn't respond, so I smile down at her as I thrust myself inside her tight pussy. She screams out loud at my brutal entrance. Wherever she has been hidden, she wasn't being touched, I'm certain of it. She's just as tight as I remember.

"It's okay," I whisper in her ear, picking up my pace. "I think I'll keep you now, anyway

Chapter 35

Kaz

'*The apartment is quiet,*' I think to myself as I wander around it aimlessly. Jonathan left earlier to run some errands. Ben is sleeping in the guestroom like he has been for the past eight hours. It's late and I know I should be tired but I can't bring myself to sleep. I'm worried about my friend, but also, I'm confused about my situation with Jamison. The asshole tried to fucking kill me. If it weren't for his brother showing up, he very well might have. I should be angry still, yet here I am contemplating this entire situation. He saved Ben. Ben told me everything. He saved my friend, and put himself in danger, when he didn't have to. I need to know why.

'*Fuck it,*' I think as I make my way towards his bedroom door. I knock once lightly, but get no response.

"Jamison?" I call out through the door, knocking again. Still no answer. Before I can talk myself out of it, I'm pushing through his bedroom door like I own the place. I'm fully expecting to be verbally assaulted, but stop short when I spot Jamison sitting at his computer desk facing away from me. He's shirtless, his tattoos on full display, and only wearing a pair of loose fitting joggers. My mouth waters. Why does this man have to be so damn sexy?

"Jamison?" I ask again, annoyed that he is ignoring me. What possible reason could he have for that? I inch closer before noticing an airpod in his ear. '*Okay, so clearly not ignoring me,*' I think to myself, suddenly a tiny bit happier. Without a second thought, I reach out to grab the airpod from his ear, when his hand lashes out and grabs my wrist hard. His chair spins around and I'm yanked onto his lap sideways, his other hand coming up to wrap around my neck.

"Did you need something, Kitten? I'm not a fan of being snuck up on," he asks me, his brow raised in question.

"I wasn't trying to sneak up on you. I knocked, but you didn't answer."

"So you decided to invade my personal space," he states matter of factly.

I shift uncomfortably on his lap. "Well, when you put it that way," I say, grimacing. "I guess that might have been an asshole move."

He smirks and removes his hands from my wrist and neck before placing one on my lower back and the other on my thigh. I'm wearing a small pair of sleep shorts, and the feel of his fingers on my bare skin sends a shot of electricity straight to my core. Without realizing I'm doing it, I wriggle my ass, grazing the semi-hard length he has beneath his joggers.

"Kitten," he growls out, his fingers digging into my skin. "Was there a point to your intrusion, because if not, I'm going to need you to leave before I do something you might not like."

"You never cared before if I liked something or not," I huff out in annoyance.

He narrows his eyes, his grip still punishing. "I always made sure you enjoyed yourself."

That comment makes me laugh out loud. This extremely smart man can hack into corporate databases and more, yet he cannot understand the difference between getting off and actually liking something. Unfortunately, somewhere down the line, everything blurred, and I actually did start enjoying our encounters. I might have even enjoyed pretending I didn't. I won't act like it started off that way, though. I'm fully aware of the psychopath who's lap I'm sitting on.

"In all seriousness, Jamison," I say, as the smile falls from my face. "Why did you save Ben?"

"Because I knew you would want him saved."

"Since when do you care what I want?" I ask him,

searching his eyes for some clue of what he is feeling.

"I care about what you want as long as it doesn't interfere with what I want," he states.

"That's bullshit," I scoff. "How would putting yourself in danger not interfere?"

"I knew it would make you happy," he says, his blue eyes darkening. I roll my eyes at him and look away, but he grabs my chin, turning me back to face him. "Did it make you happy?"

"Yes it did, but I still don't understand you," I say, perplexed. "I'm not sure I ever will. Do you care about me, Jamison, or am I just another chess piece on your board?"

He looks away from me, his jaw tense. How the hell am I ever going to get inside this enigma of a man's head? I move to get off of his lap, but he tightens his grip on me. I grab both of his hands with mine and gently move them off of me. I can tell he doesn't want to let go, but he doesn't realize I'm not going anywhere. Sliding to the ground between his legs, I place both of my hands on his thighs and look up at him. His gaze snaps to mine, his pupils completely blown. If I need to be below him in order to get him to open up to me, then that's what I'll fucking do. He leans forward, his hand gripping my chin.

"You're not a game. I...I do care." He scrunches his brows up in confusion, like he's trying to think of what he wants to say. I've never seen him look this perplexed before. It makes me feel powerful, that this man, a God in his own right, is suddenly flustered by me.

"I don't want you to leave. If I can keep you forever, I will," he says with conviction.

My heart flutters in my chest. It wasn't a love letter, but it was the closest thing I think I might ever get from him. Inside, I'm doing the happy dance, but on the outside, my eyes zero in on the bulge in his pants. The bulge that is currently eye level with me. I go to tug on his joggers, when he grips my hand to stop me. His gaze penetrates mine like he's searching for something. At first I'm confused, but then it hits me.

"I want to," I say, biting my lip. "Let me show you how

grateful I am for what you did for my friend." Relief flickers over him so quickly, you wouldn't know it was there if you weren't looking at him in that split second. He nods his head yes, and lifts his butt from the chair, allowing me to pull his joggers down. His dick springs free, already at full mast, a bead of pre-cum on the tip. I lean over and lick it before wrapping my lips over the head and sucking in. He groans in response before sliding his fingers over my head and pulling the scrunchy from my hair. My hair falls down, cascading over my shoulders, and he runs his fingers through it before holding it to the back of my head and gripping it tightly.

"Fuck, Kitten," he groans out as he uses his hands to set my pace. I hollow my cheeks out and relax my throat, allowing him to use my mouth the way I know he likes. "Such a perfect little slut for me." I moan out around him as wetness pools between my thighs. His dirty words do things to me I never thought they would. He pulls my mouth from him and lifts me quickly, pulling my shorts down, and discarding them on the floor. Before I know what's happening, he has me straddling him on the chair, his cock sinking deep inside me. He thrusts into me hard, hitting that sweet spot inside.

"Jamison, fuck, I'm going to come already," I moan out as I hold on for the ride and he thrusts into me from below. The build up is fast and before I know it, I'm clenching around him, coming undone. He continues to thrust into me while I ride out my orgasm. I'm completely in the throes of passion, my head hanging back, when I turn slightly and my eyes lock onto a pair of bright blue ones.

"Jonathan?" I say, when I see him standing in the doorway, leaning against the frame. His eyes look heated and I can't tell if he's angry or not. I mean, I know we've had a few encounters all together but we haven't officially discussed what this all means, especially after the incident at The Vault. Jonathan stalks over to me and leans down, his mouth connecting with mine in a brutal kiss, while Jamison leisurely thrusts himself inside me and sucks one of my nipples into his mouth.

"That was so fucking sexy to watch, Pretty Girl. I might need to jack off a few times in a row after that sight." He goes to turn away, but I grab his hand.

"You can stay," I say, looking to Jamison for confirmation. He nods yes.

"Tempting," Jonathan says, looking at me with lust, "but I think I'll sit this one out."

"Are you sure?" Jamison asks as Jonathan makes it to the door. There's a hint of concern in his voice and maybe a little confusion at our offer being declined.

Jonathan smiles at him. "I'm positive, brother. I think you both need this, tonight." He walks out, shutting the door behind him.

Jamison stands and grabs my ass to hold me up. His dick is still inside me as he walks us over to his bed and lays me down. He continues to thrust himself deep inside me, building me up again. He hooks one of my legs up over my shoulder, the angle heightening all of my senses. This time my orgasm sneaks up on me. I explode just as he does, his body tensing up as he seats himself fully inside me. He pulls out of me and sits back on his knees, watching with heated eyes as his cum drips out.

"Beautiful." I don't know why, but his words make me blush. There's something different about this experience tonight. Maybe something gentler…less punishing? I'm not sure what it is, but I'm not complaining.

"What are you doing?" I ask, wide eyed, as he yanks me to the edge of his bed and sinks down onto his knees between my legs. His breath is warm on my core and I'm already so sensitive. This feels more intimate. He's never done this with me before. Those nervous thoughts have me closing my legs without realizing it.

"Stop," he growls out, forcing my legs back open. "If I get to keep you, I keep all of you. You don't get to hide any part of yourself from me, Kitten." He pushes two fingers inside me, along with the cum that dripped out, before sinking his mouth down to feast. And oh my god, does he do just that. He licks and sucks me, making me squirm beneath him. I can feel the heat growing deep inside as he pays special attention to my clit, sucking it into his mouth. I was already so sensitive, but the thought of Jamison on his knees for me, lights me up from the inside. My orgasm explodes, causing me to pull his hair to keep him right where I want him as I ride it out. My thighs close around his head, holding him in a vice, yet his mouth continues its onslaught. Before I know it, my legs fall apart and I'm breathing hard, trying to push him away.

"No more," I say weakly as he licks and nibbles his way up my body. He grabs me, pulling my back to his front and the blankets up over us both.

"Fucking, perfect," he whispers, holding me tightly to him. I'm so tired I don't even have the mindset to question the fact that I'm about to fall asleep in Jamison's bed with his arms wrapped around me.

Chapter 36

Jonathan

I wake with a groan when I try to roll over and my very hard dick gets in the way.

'Fuck,' I think to myself as I roll out of bed and grip my length through my briefs. I can practically feel it pulsing, begging me for relief. Making my way to my bathroom, I turn the shower on before stripping down. My dick is hard and angry looking. It's also chaffed. I may have jerked off one too many times last night after walking in on my brother fucking Kaz. I might have even done it while standing outside of his bedroom door and listening to their moans like a fucking creeper. I'm not even sorry about it either. I step into the shower and pour some body wash onto myself before gripping my length firmly and tugging. Memories of Kaz riding him, her head thrown back in pleasure while she came all over his dick, resurface. She looked so fucking perfect, her body flushed from the intensity of her orgasm. The look in her eyes when I knew she wanted me to stay and oh how I wanted to, but I knew they needed that. They needed that moment together, just the two of them.

"Fuck, fuck," I grit out as my orgasm slams into me and my cum coats the shower wall. That was fast. I quickly clean up, before exiting the shower. The apartment is quiet as I throw on a pair of joggers and grab a t-shirt. I'm slipping it on over my head as I walk out of my bedroom when I notice Jamison sitting out on our balcony by himself. As I walk closer, I notice he doesn't have his phone or even a computer with him. Definitely not normal for him.

"Brother?" I ask, as I slide the balcony door open and

step out. He's got a far away look in his eyes, like he's thinking intensely. "Brother," I repeat, pulling a chair out next to him, "are you okay?"

His head whips around and his eyebrows scrunch up in confusion. "I'm fine."

It dawns on me then. I don't know why I didn't realize it earlier as I jump out of my chair and rush towards his room. I fling the door open quickly, frantically searching for Kaz. She sleeps peacefully on Jamison's bed, bundled up under his cover, her blonde hair splayed over the pillow. My heart rate slows when I realize she's okay. It's not that I think he would hurt her, at least not on purpose. My brother is a master at control when he's awake. It's when sleep comes, and the nightmares take over, that his true demons come out. I quietly slip from the room and make my way back out to the balcony before sitting down again.

"She slept in your bed."

He doesn't respond to me as he continues to stare out over the city.

"She slept in your bed and you didn't hurt her," I repeat. "Tell me brother, did you dream? Did the nightmares come out to play? Lie and tell me you didn't just have the best sleep of your life."

"How do you know I didn't hurt her? What makes you think I wasn't plagued with the nightmares from our past?" He grits out, still not looking me in the eye.

"I know," I say, smirking. "I know because when she's in my arms, I don't suffer either. She's like our own personal dreamcatcher, Jamison. Tell me you don't feel it. Tell me you don't care about her"

"I don't have the capacity to feel the way you do, Jonathan. You know this."

"You care about me," I state.

"You are my flesh and blood. My other half. We are one. It is not the same." he replies in a bored tone.

"What if I want her for myself then?" I ask, baiting him. His fingers grip the armrest on his chair, making me smirk.

"What if I don't want to share her anymore? Would you let me have her then? Would you give your other half this one request?"

"You know I cannot," he grits out. His knuckles are practically white with how tightly he's gripping his chair. He peers over at me with such intensity in his eyes. They narrow when he sees me still smirking at him.

"You care for her. You wouldn't give her to me anymore than you would give me to her, Brother," I say standing up and walking over to his chair.

I lean over, placing my hands around his, my face inches from his. "You love her. You may not understand it, but I see it. I feel it. She was made for us. For the both of us, and now that we have her, we can't ever let her go."

The door slides open, revealing Kaz in a loose t-shirt. "Am I interrupting something?" she asks quizzically.

"Not at all, Pretty Girl," I say standing back up and stalking towards her. She smirks when she sees me peruse her body, starting at her legs and making my way up to the hem over her shirt. I lean against her, running my fingers up the outside of her thigh. My dick is already hard again. I don't know how I'll survive with this permanent hard on I seem to have since she's been around me 24/7. I know she can feel it as I press myself up against her. "If you don't go and put some clothes on, you may end up reenacting the scene from last night, but this time your mouth will be full. She leans up to kiss me, nibbling on my lip as she pulls away and grazes her hand down the outside of the crotch of my pants.

"Mmm, tempting," she says, making me growl out when she squeezes my dick. "However, Riley just called. Sebastian and her are on their way over. They won't be more than ten minutes out." She pulls away from me quickly and walks back towards Jamison's room, whipping the t-shirt over her head in the process showing how naked she was underneath. "I need to change."

"You torture me," I say, placing my hand over my heart and making her laugh. "Just wait until they leave. I hope you got a good night's rest, Pretty Girl."

She looks back, smiling before disappearing around the corner and when I turn back towards Jamison, I find him also watching her with clear lust in his eyes.

Chapter 37

Kaz

"I knew you would contact me again, Little Devil," Lockhart purrs out, making me cringe. He swirls the straw around his drink while looking at me, hungrily. His gaze makes me sick to my stomach.

"I need money," I say.

He smiles wide, before taking a sip of his drink and leaning back in the dingy booth we are seated at. "I'm sure I could find a few ways for you to make some money." He eyes me, ogling my body, the implications clear in his eyes. I can't see Jonathan or Jamison but I can practically feel the anger radiating from them, wherever they are.

My eyes narrow on Lockhart. "You know that's not what I meant. The only place I'll be making money in the underground will be in the ring."

"Pity," he says, looking out the window first before focusing back on me. "I was hoping to find out what has both of my spawn so wrapped up in you."

Shock jolts through me but I'm hoping I don't show it outwardly. He knows I've been with both of them? What else does he know?

"You know the ring is different now," he states, pulling me from my thoughts.

I roll my eyes at him. "What? Do I have to bet money on myself? It can't be much different from before. You fight. If you win, you walk away a few bucks richer. If you lose, you walk away bruised and battered."

Lockhart laughs out loud, causing a few people to turn

our way. "It really has been a while since you've been down there, hasn't it?"

I glare at him, not appreciating the way he is mocking me.

He leans in closer, "Oh sweet girl, how things have changed. Yes, Little Devil, the winner walks away with a decent amount of money. The winner also gets to make a choice." Lockhart pauses for dramatic effect, making me want to lean over and choke the shit out of him. "If the winner so chooses, they get to fuck the loser."

I scoff before leaning back in my seat. "You're fucking with me."

"I'm not," he replies flippantly. He swirls the straw around his drink again. "The winner gets to fuck the loser right there in the ring, in front of everyone. Man, woman, it doesn't matter. It's entirely the winner's choice."

"Why the fuck would anyone agree to that?" I ask, still not quite believing what he's telling me.

"Money of course, Little Devil. You of all people would know what it's like to be desperate enough to want to escape."

I glare at him, making him laugh again. More people look our way.

"Come," he says, moving to slide out of his side of the booth. "We are drawing too much attention and I would prefer if we spoke somewhere more private."

I hesitate. I know the guys are somewhere watching and listening. They also told me not to leave with him. My job was to keep him here long enough for them to take out Lockhart's men. But if I don't get up now, he might leave before we have the chance to really get him alone. We need this. I slide out of my booth quickly and follow Lockhart outside. His car waits right outside the doors to the bar we were just in. It's as if he had this timed perfectly. My stomach lurches, causing me to wonder If I'm making a mistake, as he opens the door and ushers me inside. He slides in next to me, closing the door behind him. I look around as the car pulls forward, noting the privacy glass that separates the driver from us. The windows are all also blacked out.

"Would the pretty Little Devil still like to fight?" Lockhart purrs, putting his hand on my leg. He leans in closer to me and my entire body tenses up.

I grip his hand hard and move it off my leg before gritting out, "back up."

His eyes narrow. "We're out of sight now. You don't have to pretend anymore. I know how much you like dick. You're fucking both of them, after all. Show me why you're so special. Show me, and maybe, maybe I'll put in a good word for you in the ring.

His last sentence makes me smile. I've let this go on too long anyway and I can't stand the thought of being trapped in this car with him any longer. Besides, Jonathan and Jamison are going to punish me for leaving with Lockhart in the first place so I might as well get some satisfaction before they get a hold of me. I lean over towards Lockhart, still smiling. I can see the excitement in his eyes, the closer I get.

"That won't be necessary," I purr out. He scrunches his eyebrows in confusion so I continue. "You see, I don't need you to put in a good word when I can just call my daddy himself and ask him nicely."

"What are you talking about, girl?" He asks me with anger coating his words.

"Oh, you didn't know?" I say leaning back in my seat, pretending to make myself comfortable. "Diablo Degerson is my father. You seem to know everything. I'm surprised you didn't catch this."

"Little Devil," he whispers to himself, clearly putting two and two together.

"Makes you wonder what else you've missed, doesn't it?" I ask him, smirking.

"Oh, Little Devil," Lockhart says with a smile, making me pause. "I'm going to thoroughly enjoy making the daughter of Diablo Degerson scream." He lunges for me, wrapping his hands around my throat and squeezing tightly. Leaning in, he licks up the side of my face. "I'm going to fuck you until you bleed out around me. I may even lock you up and keep you forever." A muffled banging sounds from the back of the vehicle.

I don't have time to react because the car we are in comes to a sharp stop, causing us both to fly forward. My head hits the floorboard of the car hard enough to daze me.

"What the fuck is going on?" I hear Lockhart scream towards the privacy glass as it rolls down. I see his eyes go wide, making me whip my head up to look at what he's seeing. Jonathan climbs through from the front seat just as the door to the car is ripped open and Jamison is reaching in to pull Lockhart out.

Chapter 38

Jamison

I rip Lockhart out of the back of the car and toss him onto the ground. Sebastian and Xavier both stand behind him, their arms crossed.

"You little shit," he says, getting to his feet and dusting off his suit.

"Hello, Father," I purr out. He visibly cringes.

"Yeah, hey, dad," Jonathan says as he climbs out from the car and helps Kaz out from behind him. She looks dazed as I scan her body for injuries.

"She's fine, just a little beat up," Jonathan says to me. I nod back at him.

"What the fuck is this about?" Lockhart asks, looking around. His eyes widen when he spots Sebastian and then Xavier.

Xavier smiles and gives a little wave. "It's like one big fucking family reunion, Uncle. Aren't you excited? Maybe we should video chat with Sasha too."

Lockhart laughs, "Oh yes, do put Sasha on a video chat for me. I would love to speak with her and tell her all about her surprise. There's someone that's been missing her and he can't wait to see her again. As a matter of fact, he's probably already there."

Xavier frowns at him before pulling his phone out and shooting off a text.

"I have a better idea," Sebastian says, causing Lockhart's head to swivel towards him. "Let's play a game."

He pulls out a revolver and empties out all of the bullets

into his hand before pocketing them and placing just one back in the chamber. He then spins it before closing it and pointing at Lockharts knee. "How about twenty questions?"

"I'll start," Xavier says, pocketing his phone. "Why did you kill your own brother?"

I raise my eyebrows at Xavier in surprise. Talk about going straight for it.

"I wanted to take over our father's empire. He would have ran it into the ground. He had too many 'feelings'," he says, making air quotes with his fingers. "The little shit was everyone's favorite. Always getting whatever the fuck he wanted. He wanted to run off into the sunset with his friends like a third fucking wheel." He turns to Jonathan and smiles before looking at me. "Sound familiar? The apples might not fall so far from the tree after all."

"Shut the fuck up," Jonathan says. "We are nothing like you. We would never hurt each other."

Lockharts smirks, not taking his eyes off of me, "says the one with all those feelings."

I glare at him.

"It's not a coincidence, we all ended up in college together. It can't be coincidence that both Riley and Kaz ended up at Bolt Corporation either. How the fuck did you swing that?" Sebastian asks from out of nowhere.

"Wouldn't you like to know?" Lockhart says, goading him.

Sebastian doesn't hesitate before pulling the trigger, making Lockhart jump.

"Should we try that again?" Sebastian asks, raising his eyebrow.

Lockhart puts his hands up to stop him, "I may have had a part with Riley applying to Bolt Corporation. I might have planted the bug in Nate's father's ear in hopes that she would get a job there so I could eventually get information on you when I took her. I didn't think you would fall for the little bitch. She was supposed to be mine to sell."

Sebastian growls and pulls the trigger. This time the gun

goes off and the bullet hits Lockhart in the knee causing him to buckle and cry out when he hits the ground.

"What the fuck?" He screams. "I answered your fucking question, you prick!"

"I know. I didn't like your answer though," Sebastian says, shrugging his shoulders and pulling out all of the remaining bullets from his pocket before replacing them back in the chamber. He hands the gun to Xavier. "This game is boring now."

Xavier takes it and points it at Lockhart. "You weren't ever going to let Sasha and I go, were you?"

Lockhart laughs. It's strained and you can tell he's in pain. "You, yes. You signed all I needed from you over. Sasha however, has always been my golden ticket to taking over The Triad. I was preparing to set up an arranged marriage for her until you came along and fucked everything up. Don't worry though, I'm sure her little friend will be seeing her very soon."

The gun goes off, hitting Lockhart in the shoulder. He howls out in pain before pressing his hand to the wound.

"How long have you been watching Kaz?" Jonathan asks as he walks over and grabs the gun from Xavier's hand.

"Long enough to know you two have been fucking her. Long enough to see that she has turned both of my spawn into weak little bitches. You're both fucking pathetic, letting some whore.."

His words are cut off by Kaz's fist connecting with his jaw. Blood flies from his mouth and his head whips sideways making both Jonathan and I grin in unison.

"Fuck, Pretty Girl," Jonathan says, adjusting himself. "That made me so fucking hard."

I look down to see the blood has indeed rushed down to my dick. "I concur, Kitten. That was sexy as fuck."

She looks at both of us, smiling wide.

"As much as I would love to watch this little show, we should probably take care of this situation first, preferably before the police show up and wonder what a bunch of lawyers are doing torturing someone," Xavier cuts in.

"How did you find out about Jonathan and I? Did you know we had been to The Cellar?" I ask. I wasn't going to but I know now, that if I don't, I might always wonder.

He spits out a glob of blood and smirks at me. The blood coats his teeth, disgustingly. His eyes dart towards his car before flicking back towards me. Is he thinking about trying to escape because if so, he is out of luck. There's no escaping this time.

"If I would have known you both were mine, I would have made sure you spent a little more time in The Cellar. Maybe then, you might have been a bit more compliant, like your cousin."

"Do you fucking care about anyone?" Kaz cuts in. She kicks him in the gut causing him to double over. "They are your fucking children, you piece of shit."

He glares at her. "They should have never been born. Had I known their mother was pregnant, I would have cut them from her stomach myself."

I look at Jonathan. It's clear Lockhart's words are affecting him. I couldn't care less what he has to say. His words are empty and meaningless to me. They make me feel nothing. Seeing my brother hurt is what guts me. Knowing he will never be able to shut off those emotions. Knowing that he will forever more carry that pain around with him. And the worst part…knowing I couldn't save him from any of it. But now…now I can.

"Enough," I say, snatching the gun from Jonathan's hand and pointing it directly in Lockhart's face.

His eyes go wide but he quickly schools his features before smirking. "Are you going to do what I did? Are you going to kill me? How about your brother? Will he be next?"

I don't say a word as I stare down at him. He really is the pathetic one. Trying so hard to control his emotions, they're practically flowing out with the blood he is losing. He's attempting to bait me into keeping him alive longer. What a ridiculous notion. The thought makes me chuckle out loud. The sound is foreign and disturbing, even to me. And when I look around, I can see the perplexed look on everyone else's faces. They too are just as surprised to hear it.

I smile wide as I approach Lockhart and bend down so I am level with him. My hand grips his hair tightly while I position the gun angled right up under his chin.

"Like father, like son," I reply before pulling the trigger.

Silence surrounds us all while I stay kneeling in front of Lockhart's mangled body. His blood coats my face, my hands and even my suit.

"I'm calling Antonio for cleanup," Sebastian says. Xavier mumbles something but I don't hear what it is. I feel soft hands come down on my shoulders before making their way up towards my face. Kaz turns my head to hers, searching my eyes. I feel my brother's hand come down on my shoulder and I instinctively grab it, holding tightly. I need something to ground me right now.

"Are you okay?" Kaz asks me.

I look down to see her hands now coated in blood and it does something to me. Leaning in, I kiss her hard. My hand comes up to her hair, gripping it firmly as I pull her closer to me and ravage her mouth. She moans into me, causing my dick to stir to life. I feel Jonathan's hand squeeze mine tighter. I'm two seconds away from taking her right here on the ground, next to Lockhart's dead body, when Xavier's voice cuts in.

"Umm, hey guys, as hot as this is to watch, I think we may have a bigger problem."

We all look over to see Sebastian walking over to Xavier who has the trunk of the car open and is peering inside with wide eyes.

"Indeed," Sebastian says, before looking at all three of us.

All three of us get up and walk over to see what the fuss is about. Inside is a tied up woman. Her mouth is taped shut and her bright blue eyes stare up at us like a deer caught in headlights. Her brown hair is a mess of tangles and she's covered in blood and bruises. Her clothing is ripped and stained.

"Jesus Christ, get her out!" Kaz yells, breaking us all out of our stupor.

Sebastian pulls her to a sitting position while I use my

pocket knife to cut her binds. Kaz gently pulls the tape from her mouth and pushes her hair from her face.

"You're safe now," she says to her. My brows scrunch up as I stare at the woman. She looks familiar. Have I seen her somewhere before?

"What's your name?" Sebastian asks. He too is looking at her oddly.

"Eve," she croaks out. Her voice sounds small and weak.

"Holy shit," Xavier whispers, loud enough for all of us to hear. "You're the woman in the picture."

"What are you talking about?" Jonathan asks him, confused.

"She's your...she's both of your..." He's looking at us both now.

I turn to see Kaz look at Jonathan and me and then Eve before her eyes go wide.

Eve turns to us both. A small weak smile forming on her lips. "Your mother.

Chapter 39

Jonathan

"Mother?" I say out loud, testing the name on my lips. I look at Jamison who stares at her quizzically. No doubt he's analyzing her entire face right now. He can see it as well as I can. Her features, so similar to ours, yet more feminine.

"We need to get her to a hospital," Kaz states, as Xavier and Sebastian help her from the trunk.

Eve shakes her head quickly. "No, no hospitals."

"But you're hurt," Xavier replies, eyeing her up and down. "You should be checked out."

Eve shakes her head no again.

"I'll call for an in-home visit," Sebastian cuts in. "We need to get out of here though before anyone sees us."

That statement pulls me from my thoughts, causing me to peer over at Lockhart's dead body. Some luck Jamison and I both have. Shitty adoptive parents and an even shittier biological father. I look back at Eve and watch as my friends help her to the car. We are running on about a twenty-five percent chance that she is just as shitty. Normally, I'm the one with a little more optimism, but fuck, I can't even bring myself to be hopeful right now. After all, this woman did give us up and disappear.

"What do you think?" I ask Jamison as we ride back separately from everyone else.

He continues driving, his face completely impassive for a good few minutes before deciding to answer me. "I think she is telling the truth. We have some of her features, although she doesn't look as if she's aged at all."

"Where do you think she has been all of this time?"

He looks over at me quickly before facing forward again. "Be careful, brother. Don't ask questions you might not want answers to."

I scrunch my eyebrows together in annoyance at my brother. This is what he does. He treats me like I'm fragile. Like I'm so much younger than him. "I do want fucking answers."

He sighs. "I just don't want you to get your hopes up. This woman…our mother just happens to show up out of nowhere. It's too convenient."

I nod my head and look out the window knowing he is probably right. Aside from our close friends, everyone in our life has always wanted something from us. What's to say Eve will be any different.

Chapter 40

Kaz

I sit in Jonathan's room and wait for Eve to finish cleaning herself up. Thankfully, Xavier and Sebastian were smart enough to call Riley and Corrine and ask them to bring over some spare clothes for Eve. The doctor had arrived at the same time as us and at first Eve had refused to be looked at. With a little convincing from me, she had finally relented and let him take a look at her. I can't imagine what this woman has had to endure, being with Lockhart. Who knows how long he had her or the unimaginable things he put her through. My thoughts take me to Jonathan and Jamison who are currently in the living room with everyone else. They have both been unusually quiet. I haven't had a chance to speak to either of them but since we returned, they have barely spoken two words to anyone, Eve included. Jonathan can barely look at her and Jamison, well, he was staring right through her.

My thoughts are interrupted by the sound of the bathroom door opening. I look up to see Eve standing there with the loose t-shirt and leggings that the girls brought for her. Her hair is washed and so is the rest of her body. It's hard to imagine her being a mother to the two men I've been sleeping with. She doesn't look a day over thirty. She's actually very beautiful in an innocent way. Suddenly I'm a little self conscious. What if she doesn't like me? I'm not exactly the girl next door type, however hard I've tried to pretend to be for all these years.

"Who are you to them?" she asks softly.

"To who?"

"My boys. I saw the way they were looking at you. The way

they both can't keep their eyes from straying to you, even at a time like this. They both care for you."

I blush and look down at my hands, unable to find an answer for her. At least one where I'm sure she won't think I'm absolutely insane. The bed dips beside me and I feel her hand wrap around one of mine. I look up, startled at her touch, but she isn't looking at me. She's looking out the window.

"A long time ago, I remember seeing that exact same look on my own face when I would look in the mirror. You don't need to be ashamed. You love them both. The difference for your situation is that those feelings are reciprocated." She looks over at me and smiles, squeezing my hand. "I have barely been here and I can already see it. I'm so glad, they have someone who cares for them the way you do."

I look over to see Jonathan standing in his doorway, watching us. Eve turns at the same time I do.

"I think it's time I explain where I've been all this time," she says, letting go of my hand and standing up and heading towards the living room. She smiles up at Jonathan before heading past him to take a seat on one of the couches. Jonathan grabs my hand and we follow out there where he pulls me down to sit between him and Jamison. Both of their hands immediately slide onto each of my thighs, causing me to shift around nervously. Both Corrine and Riley smirk at me but nobody else says a word. Maybe this situation won't be quite as weird as I thought it would be.

"I'm going to start from the beginning," Eve says. And she does. Everyone pitches in, filling in bits and pieces of information. Riley and Corrine talk about their parents and finding pictures with Eve in them. Xavier talks about his parents as well. The wistful look in Eve's eye is obvious when his father is mentioned. She tells us about Lockhart and the vile things he did. About her parents finding out she was pregnant. Apparently, her parents and Lockhart's made a deal behind her back. They were paid off to move away and disappear. Her parents whisked her away out of the country to finish out her pregnancy. Once the babies were born, she was forced to give them up for adoption and when she attempted to run with them, her parents had her committed. She remained locked up until recently when she was released.

"I don't understand," I say, confused. "How did you end up back here?"

"That's just it," she replies. "I have no idea how I was released. One day, they just came and told me I was free to go. I was told my parents had both passed away and given an account with an extremely large sum of money in it. There was already a plane ticket purchased from the account, to bring me back here. When my flight landed, a taxi was waiting to bring me to an already furnished and stocked apartment. I didn't leave for an entire week because I didn't know where to go or what to do. The truth is, it's been so long since I've been out in the real world, I wasn't really sure how to do anything anymore. All I knew is I wanted to find my boys." She looks over at Jonathan and Jamison, smiling with tears in her eyes. "I wanted them to know, I never would have given them up, had I had a choice."

They both stare at her uncomfortably. I'm sure they have no idea how to react to this situation so I squeeze their hands to let them know I'm here for them. It's not a lot, but the slight squeeze they both give me, lets me know they are grateful.

"Lockhart," Riley pipes in. "How did he get a hold of you?"

"I'm...I'm not really sure. All I know is some men showed up to my apartment one day and grabbed me when I opened the door. When they dropped me off in front of Ethan, all he kept talking about was DNA Paperwork and accusing me of sending it to him."

"So you didn't send him anything?" Jamison asks suddenly.

Eve looks at him with sad eyes. "No, I never would have done that. I knew how horrible he was when we were younger and although I couldn't have known how bad he was now, I never would have wanted to put you both anywhere near him."

Jamison dips his head to her, in an acknowledgment of

what she says. I can tell he believes her.

"So Lockhart is really gone?" Corrine asks, from beside Xavier.

"He's dead, Butterfly. He won't be able to hurt any of us ever again," Xavier replies, hugging her close to him. I see Sebastian hug Riley tight to him as well. The room is silent while we all revel in the fact that Lockhart can no longer hurt us.

"I know I don't deserve it," Eve says, breaking the silence. "But, if you could find it in your hearts to forgive me for not finding a way to you both sooner, I would really like to be a part of your lives. I want to get to know you." She looks from Jamison to Jonathan, before settling on me and finishing her sentence. "All of you."

"It wasn't your fault," I say, barely above a whisper. I glance at the men on either side of me, squeezing their hands. They both look at each other before nodding and turning to stare at their mother.

"I think Jamison and I can both agree, we would like that as well, Jonathan states, squeezing my hand back. I look at Jamison, waiting for him to say something, anything, in this moment and when he does, my heart fills with excitement.

"We would," are the only words that escape from his lips but it's enough to know he means them.

The sound of a phone ringing jolts the entire room. Jamison pulls a cell phone out of his pocket and peers at the screen, his eyebrow furrowed.

"It's Lockhart's phone. The caller ID says T3."

Chapter 41

Jamison

"Yes," I say, answering the call and placing it on speaker. I motion for everyone else to be silent.

"Cellar," a voice states before a second voice repeats him.

"Who the fuck is this?" I ask, irritably.

"Who are you?" Voice two asks.

Voice one cuts him off with a growl. "Don't answer that fucking question. The Triad do not reveal themselves."

"Is he dead?" Voice two asks.

"If you're asking if Lockhart is dead," I reply in a bored tone. "I blew his head off earlier today."

Somebody hisses over the line while the other chuckles.

"Do you know of the Triad? Do you know of the rules? You kill one of us, you take our place."

"And if I refuse?" I ask, casually leaning back into the couch.

"Refusal isn't an option." Voice one states.

"The way I see it, you don't know me, so refusal doesn't sound so bad. I want nothing to do with The Cellar," I grit out.

"You don't know what you're doing!" Voice two exclaims. "You will disrupt The Triad. There must always be three. You are putting many others in jeopardy."

"I don't give a fuck. Lockhart is dead. If you call this number again, I will make sure your so-called Triad dies too. I will make my way back to The Cellar, and this time, I will make sure the entire place burns to the ground."

"So you refuse?" Voice one asks.

I look around the room to see everyone staring at me,

anticipating what I will say next before speaking back into the phone. "I refuse."

"You have no idea what you have just done," voice two responds before the line goes dead.

"Well, that was ominous," Jonathan pipes in jokingly.

Xavier laughs, "I don't know about you guys, but I think we should celebrate. Lockhart is dead. Who gives a fuck what happens to The Triad now."

"Yes!" Corrine and Riley both respond together.

Kaz looks up at me with soft eyes before turning to my brother.

"I think I agree," Jonathan says, looking from Kaz to me. "A celebration is in order. How about the club next weekend, Xavier? I heard there's going to be another masked event."

Corrine giggles and looks at Riley, who turns a bright shade of red.

"Little Mouse," Sebastian whispers in her ear. "I know how much you love wearing a mask."

Everyone bursts out laughing, except for Eve, who is completely in the dark. Kaz takes it upon herself to tell her the story, making Eve giggle as well. Eventually Kaz and Ben move to the patio by themselves. I want so badly to grab her and take her to my room, hiding her from everyone. It takes everything in my power not to steal her away but I know she needs this. If Ben was into women, she most certainly wouldn't be out there with him, alone. My patience can only go so far. I make arrangements for Ben to stay with Sebastian and Riley while Eve stays with us. I've already put in the call for an available apartment in our building for Ben but I will have to call in the morning for a second one for Eve.

After what feels like hours, everyone finally leaves and I watch as Kaz helps my mother to Jonathan's room giving her a place to sleep for the evening. I'm at my computer, with Jonathan casually sitting up in my bed, when Kaz returns. She hovers by the door nervously causing me to look up from my work.

"Are you sure this is okay?" She gestures to my bed with Jonathan laying in it.

"You have been in my bed already, Kitten," I say with a smirk.

Her hands are clasped together and she's moving her fingers back and forth, looking down at them. "Yes but, umm, not all of us together."

I motion for her to go to my bed and follow behind her. Jonathan pulls the covers back allowing her to slide in beside him. She lays her head on his chest as I slide in behind her and wrap my arm around her. My brother kisses Kaz's forehead gently. The motion makes me grateful he's here with us. My other half. His light, my dark and her softness.

'It could never be any other way,' I think, as Jonathan turns the light off and slides down under the covers. His arm wraps over mine, encasing Kaz between us, as we all drift off to sleep together.

Chapter 42

Jonathan

We went out to Lock & Key tonight to celebrate with everyone. It was Jamison who eventually suggested we secure a hotel room for tonight. It's been a little over a week since Eve, our mother, came into the picture. Although we've each spent time separately with Kaz, we really haven't gotten a chance to all be together again. Since we've been having our mother stay with us, we thought it better to not have any crazy escapades with her in hearing distance. Our place is large but it's certainly not soundproof. I've been working on securing an apartment for her in our building, that way she can still be close, but we won't be able to move her into it for a few more weeks. She did try to tell us she could go back to hers but neither Jamison and I were having it. The apartment she was in was a shithole, and there's no way we are letting her live somewhere like that. Kaz had lunch with her father, his wife and her half brother this week. I didn't go with but Jamison did. She seemed so happy to have finally met them. Later, Jamison told me her father would make for good business prospects. Leave it to my brother to focus solely on that. When I asked about her stepmother and half brother he told me that her brother was an egotistical and pompous little prick and the stepmother was an alcoholic housewife. That last part made me laugh out loud. I guess nobody's family is as perfect as they want to make themselves seem. As for Kaz's best friend, Ben, he actually seems to be a great guy. Not only is he super smart, he's extremely tech savvy. He must have impressed my brother quite a bit, because he is currently getting ready to start working for our IT department.

Either that, or he hired him for Kaz's benefit. I don't think he would admit to either to be quite honest. All I really care about is that he is happy. Kaz is happy. If they are, then so am I.

I stumble into the hotel room drunkenly, pulling Kaz behind me. Jamison chuckles as he follows behind us, locking the door. I watch as my brother whispers in Kaz's ear from behind causing her to smile and blush. She looks so fucking happy. Happier than I've ever seen her and I love it. My brother looks up at me, smirking deviously as he pushes one of Kaz's straps off her shoulder.

"Look at Jonathan, Kitten," he whispers in her ear, loud enough for me to hear. "Look at how hungry he is for you." He slips her other strap down and I hear the sound of her zipper coming undone as I approach. Her dress falls around her feet leaving her completely nude underneath.

"Commando?" I ask, raising my eyebrow.

"Jamison stole my panties earlier tonight at the club," she answers breathlessly, as my brother nibbles on her neck. I drop to my knees in front of her and swipe my fingers across her pussy.

"Have you been wet for us all night, Pretty Girl?" I ask, when my fingers come away slick. "Have you been dripping and making a mess between your thighs?"

"Yes," she replies, her eyes heated as she looks down at me. Jamison hooks his arm under one of her legs and lifts it up, opening her up to me completely.

"Let my brother taste you, Kitten. Tell him how bad you want him." He pinches her nipples causing her body to rock out closer to me.

"Fuck, I want you," she moans out. "I want you both."

I lean in and lick her gently and she grabs my head and rocks her pussy against my mouth, making me smile.

Jamison chuckles and continues to pinch her nipples. "Such a greedy little slut, aren't you? Look at you riding Joanthan's face. You can't get enough of it."

And fuck, he's not wrong. Kaz pulls my face closer,

rubbing her pussy against my mouth while I continue to devour her. It doesn't take long before I feel her body spasm and she pulses against my tongue. My brother holds her as her body goes limp in his arms before they both drop to their knees.

"I fucking love you, Pretty Girl," I whisper before kissing her hard. She pulls back from me and runs her fingers across my lips before whispering back.

"I love you too, Jonathan."

Chapter 43

Jamison

"Show Jonathan how much you love him and return the favor," I say, as I smoothly press down on her neck. Jonathan removes his clothes quickly, his dick springing free. Kaz looks back at me, biting her lip, before turning and sucking him deep into her mouth. He hisses out and runs his fingers through her hair, holding her head and gently guiding her. I remove my clothes quickly, stroking my hard dick, as I watch Kaz bob her head up and down. Kaz yelps when I smack her ass hard, but she doesn't have time to pull back and look at me. I lean over her quickly speaking in her ear as I rub my dick against her entrance.

"My brother may be soft with you, but I know how much you like it rough too. This is why you want us both, isn't it, Kitten?" She gags when I push her head down on Jonathan's dick, but it turns into a moan as I press the head of my cock just barely inside her entrance. She wiggles her ass back against me, needing more. Jonathan pulls her mouth from his dick.

"Say it again, Pretty Girl. Tell us you want us."

"I want you both," she says breathlessly.

"Only us?" I ask, leaning over and biting her shoulder.

"Fuck. Yes. Both of you. Only the both of you," she whispers before sucking Jonathan back into her mouth.

As soon as those words leave her mouth, I slide myself inside her in one swift motion. She pulls away slightly at the quick intrusion, but I've got a tight hold on both of her hips. She's not going anywhere. Fuck, she's so fucking tight and wet and perfect. I could do this every day for the rest of my life, if she let me. I slam into her, feeling her start to tighten up around me in anticipation of an impending orgasm. She's so close, I can feel it. My thumb slides into my mouth before pressing against her ass. I feel her tense as I gently prod her, slowly moving just the tip in and out. It's not long before she's backing herself up against me.

"Fuck, that's so hot, Pretty Girl. I'm so close. Be a good girl and swallow me for me, okay?" Jonathan says, guiding her head up and down. She moans something unintelligible.

"Wait for it brother," I tell him. He nods his head, gritting his teeth as I slide my other hand around her and press against her clit. The motion causes my thumb to press further inside her. Her pussy tightens around me and I pump inside her and within seconds she's exploding.

"Fuck," Jonathan yells out as Kaz moans so loud, she practically swallows his dick down her throat. "Fuck, fuck, Pretty Girl, take it all."

As soon as she's done I grab her by her throat and pull her back up against my front, continuing to pump furiously inside her. Jonathan leans over, sucking one of her nipples into his mouth and rubbing her clit with his fingers. She moans again, holding onto him for dear life.

"Come for us again, Kitten," I growl out. And she does. She comes again just as I empty myself inside her, biting down on her shoulder hard enough to leave a mark.

She's like putty in my hands as I lift her in my arms and walk into the bathroom, setting her on the counter. Jonathan turns the water on in the large walk in shower for us and proceeds to adjust the temperature.

"You," I say, standing between her legs and grabbing her chin so she's looking directly at me. "Both of you," I reiterate as I look back at my brother and then into Kaz's eyes. "You are everything to me."

Chapter 44

Kaz

"I love you too, Jamison," I say, as I stare up at him. He may not have said those exact words, but I know that's what he meant. I can feel it. This connection between the three of us. It's like something inside of us has been unlocked. The entire world could fade away, but the three of us, we will always be.

He smiles at me before kissing me hard. It's a real smile too. The kind of smile only meant for Jonathan and I to see. He grabs me off the counter before carrying me to the shower where Jonathan is waiting. The door closes behind us and steam immediately fills the shower. I can already feel how hard Jamison is again as my pussy rubs against him while we kiss. Jonathan is hard as steel behind me as he kisses my back, my shoulders, my neck. These men are insatiable, but you know what? So am I. I don't know if I'll ever get enough. I feel Jamison lift me slightly before sliding me back down onto him, his hard length filling me to the brim.

"More, I need more," I say, as I rock against him. "I need you both inside me."

Jamison looks at Jonathan over my shoulder and nods before lifting me and letting his dick slide out. The sudden emptiness has me yearning for more but is quickly gone when I feel Jonathan slide himself inside me. They work together to hold me up while Jonathan pumps himself inside my pussy, coating his dick with my wetness. He pulls out and Jamison enters me again before pulling me closer to him and spreading me for his brother. I feel the head of Jonathan's dick push slightly into my ass and immediately tense up.

"Breathe, Kitten," Jamison whispers as he holds me with one arm and thumbs my clit between us. He kisses me deeply, relaxing my body enough for Jonathan to slip further inside.

I whine out between them, from pain, or pleasure, I'm not sure. Maybe a mixture of both. All I know is I don't want it to stop.

"I'm almost there, Pretty Girl," Jonathan grits out. Jamison flicks my clit again, causing me to rock back and push against Jonathan. The motion has us all moaning in unison as they both become fully seated inside of me.

"Fuck, it's so full," I cry out as they both slide out the smallest bit before pressing back inside. They pump inside me in tandem, sending me over the edge immediately. I pulse and pulse around them, not knowing where one orgasm ends and another begins as they both hit those perfect spots. My body is on fire. By the time they both empty themselves inside of me, I've lost count of how many times I've come. When we finish and finally all catch our breath, they both proceed to wash my body before drying me off and carrying me to the bedroom. Jamison slides in first while Jonathan places me on the bed, allowing me to crawl to the middle. Once I'm settled in, my head on Jamison's chest, Jonathan cuddles up and spoons me from behind.

"Well that was a great ending to our night," I say, giggling.

"Just wait until the morning, Pretty Girl," Jonathan responds while squeezing me.

"If I wake up, and your dick is anywhere near me," Jamison growls out. "I will cut it off."

"Ouch, where is the love, brother?" Jonathan jokes.

"If it's a problem, we could put pajamas on before we fall asleep," I suggest, innocently.

"No," both men say in unison, making me laugh out loud.

Eventually, I fall asleep to the sounds of the city and the soft caresses of the two men who complete me in more ways than I can imagine. I know, in my heart, I wouldn't have it any other way.

Epilogue

Jonathan

Two Weeks Later

"Have you spoken to Andre recently?" I ask Sebastian as we all sit down for our meeting.

Sebastian leans back in his chair, moving around some files. "No actually, I was going to ask you the same thing. We both look up to find Jamison and Xavier walking into the room. They sit down, both staring at us quizzically.

"Did we walk in on something spicy?" Xavier jokes. My brother smirks but doesn't say anything. I see a smudge of lipstick on his collarbone. It's peeking out from where his suit collar normally covers. No one else would notice, except for me, because it matches the exact shade of red Kaz has been wearing lately.

'Lucky bastard,' I think to myself, while I stare at the mark. I've been stuck in a previous meeting with Sebastian and a client while that fucker obviously had the time of his life with our Pretty Girl. My phone suddenly vibrating in my pocket, pulls me out of my trance.

Unlocking the screen, I see a message pop through from Jamison and when I open it, I immediately groan under my breath. I look up to see him smirking at me and my thumb must slip because the sound of Kaz moaning and skin slapping immediately begins to play.

"Fuck yes!" Xavier says, reaching for my phone. "You know I can't resist good porn."

My eyes go wide and I watch in slow motion as Xavier's

hand moves toward my phone and Jamison reaches over, slapping it away with a growl.

"What the fuck?" Xavier asks, clearly confused.

Sebastian scoots his chair in and places his hands under his chin. "We are supposed to be in a fucking meeting with our phones silenced. Forgive me if I don't feel like ever hearing my head of HR moan like that again."

Like a lightbulb went off, Xavier immediately smiles wide.

"That was Kaz? Oh shit!" He turns towards my brother, "sorry man, I didn't realize."

"It's fine," Jamison clips. "What were you two discussing when we walked in?"

Sebastian gets the video call ready while speaking. "We were talking about how we haven't heard from Andre in a few days."

"Well, I know Sasha told me last week there was some weird stuff going on with the internet and electricity there. Maybe that's the problem," Xavier states.

"A problem with phone service as well?" It's more of a rhetorical question as Sebastain gestures to the video call that won't go through to Andre. I pull my phone out quickly and try to place a regular call to Andre but it sends me straight to voicemail.

"Try calling Sasha. His call went to voicemail."

Xavier whips his phone out next and dials, placing it on speaker. I see my brother already on his phone out of the corner of my eye. The call to Sasha also goes straight to voicemail causing my stomach to churn.

"Maybe it is the phone service too?" Xavier says, lifting his hands up to his hair and running his fingers through. I can tell he's already stressed out.

"They don't have the same cell service," Sebastian states. "Do you think Andre's father would really let him walk around with shitty service? Something is wrong."

"Indeed," my brother says out loud, his face still buried in his phone. Our heads swivel his direction, waiting for whatever it is he just figured out.

He looks up at all of us, a clear look of uncertainty on his face. "Their tracking locations are gone. It's as if they've both completely disappeared."

Stay up to date on the release of the final book in *The Men of Bolt Corporation* Series by subscribing to my newsletter!
Subscribe

Keep a lookout for more novels in the future from your favorite side characters in this series!
If you haven't yet, come and join our Facebook reader group!
Facebook

Author Note

Hey you! Yes, I'm talking to all of you! I'm so fucking grateful for every single person who has made it this far in the world of Bolt Corporation! I love every one of you who have supported me on this crazy roller coaster. I'm thankful for my friends and family, especially those of you who read my books even though you don't like reading! You didn't have to, but you did, and that means so much to me! Lastly, I gotta thank my four Alphas who made this book legible for all of you. Sarah, Samantha, Maggie and Jaycee…You guys are fucking rockstars!
Now onto Andre and Sasha's story in Book Four, which will complete the series.
Don't worry, there's a few side characters who will get their own novels soon too!
XOXO K.A. Wombolt

Made in the USA
Columbia, SC
28 January 2025